Hal's

Worldly

Temptations

By Fay Risner

Cover Art

By Fay Risner 2/2011
All Rights reserved

Published by Fay Risner
Publisher Booksbyfay Publishing
fayrisner@netins.net
Nursing Consultant Tracy Hanson RN

To All My Readers

Thank you to all the readers of my Nurse Hal Among The Amish Series for sticking with me. I hope you enjoy this next chapter in Nurse Hal's life, Hal's Worldly Temptations, and continue to look for future books about her and the Lapp family.

Sincerely,

Fay Risner

And they called Rebekah and said unto her,
"Wilt thou go with this man?"
And she said, "I will go."
Genesis 24:58

Reviews about my books

A Promise Is A Promise-Book 1- Nurse Hal AmongThe Amish

- Growing up in the Mid West I loved the style and tone of the story and scenery. No purple prose or overly nostalgic descriptions but rather a simple and honest portrayal of daily life. Each character is original and thoughtfully developed. I whole heartedly enjoyed this Amish tale and believed the contrast between the Plain and English, but also how it is possible to live together with understanding, honesty and acceptance. The story is not overtly religious but rather focuses on the complexities of relationships and because of this drew me into the Lapp family. www.bitsybling.wordpress.com

Christmas Traditions

- If you like Margaret Yoder in The Rainbow's End you should read Christmas Traditions the first book about her life.
- This review is from Authornomy.com
- This book is an informative piece from a human interest point of view. Your writing is atmospheric and your narrative comes across as natural, believable and very vivid.
- Review from www.authornomy.com

Chapter 1

Bacon! Hal pulled the sheet off her chin, wrinkled her nose and sniffed. Greasy, stomach rolling, strong smelling bacon. Whether she liked it or not that's what she smelled. Hal pressed one hand against her crazily pitching, queasy stomach and used the other to pull the sheet up over her nose to try to block the stink.

Mom must be cooking breakfast. She blinked her eyes and rubbed them, trying to wake up. A peek from one eye at the window told her it was still dark outside. What was Mom doing up this early? She glanced at the clock beside the bed and groaned softly. Three scarlet numbers, four and two zeros glared at her.

Hal grabbed her bathrobe and slipped into it on the way to the kitchen. She put her hands on her hips and studied her stocky, gray haired mother's back as she stood in of the cookstove. "Mom, do you know what time it is? I'd hoped I could sleep in a little longer. We've got a lot of work to do today to get ready for my wedding tomorrow. What are you doing up this early?"

"From what your Aunt Tootie found in a book about the Amish at the library, they always get up early. We need to get a move on so we get to the farm fairly soon. We don't want the Lapp family to think we're lazy people. You might as well get used to getting out of bed before daylight," Nora Lindstrom chided.

"I don't think they get up this early," groaned Hal.

Nora forked the bacon from the skillet onto a plate. "You sure? Maybe we should ask John so you know for sure."

1

"No, don't bother," Hal said brusquely and changed the subject. "No breakfast for me, Mom. I don't think I could eat a bit,"

Nora focused a knowing smile on her daughter. "Didn't fix you any. This is for your dad. I'm not so old that I don't remember my wedding day. Didn't think you'd be able to eat much today or tomorrow until after the wedding is over. The coffee's done if you want a cup."

"Sure. That I need to wake me up," Hal said dryly. As she poured, she said, "Thanks, Mom, for helping me box up my things last night. It won't take long to clear out the apartment now. I know that was a chore you didn't expect as soon as you arrived yesterday. You had to be tired after that long drive from Titonka."

"Wasn't that big a job. I was glad to help." Nora broke two eggs into the hot greasy skillet.

"I cleaned out my closet before I went to bed and sacked my clothes to give Good Will. We can put them in the drop off box this morning on the way out of town," Hal said, staring off into space.

The sound in Hal's voice made Nora twist to study her. "You don't sound so all right about giving away your clothes."

"That is hard. I like my English clothes, but when I think about choosing between a fashion statement and a family, there's no contest," Hal said, sitting down at the table with her coffee. "I've one box of photo albums I'd like Dad to put in the car trunk so you don't go off without it. You might as well take the pictures home with you. I hate to throw them away."

"I get it that the Amish don't want pictures taken of them," Nora started. "But ----."

"They think when someone takes a picture of them that's stealing their soul. The bible says no graven images," Hal interrupted.

"I know all that, but you weren't Amish when those pictures were taken. I'd think you could at least take the small album with your grandparents, parents, aunts and uncles in it to your new home. Someday John's children and hopefully, some of

2

your own would like to see what you looked like as a child and their ancestors."

"You think?" Hal said optimistically.

Her mother's head, brown hair feathered with gray, nodded. She had her attention on the eggs she was turning. "Can't see how it would be bad to have pictures of people who didn't believe the graven image scripture. John and his family should be broad minded enough to allow you your family pictures."

"You're right, Mom. I hate to give that album up. The school pictures, it doesn't really bother me to not ever see again. All right, I'll slip the small album in with the bedding and tuck it away in a drawer for the future. Thanks, Mom."

"You're welcome." Nora turned her head toward the hallway and yelled, "Jim, get out here and eat. Your breakfast is ready." The toaster banged. Two pieces of toast shot up. Further warning breakfast was about to be served whether Jim was ready or not. Nora buttered each slice before she scooted them on a plate beside the bacon and hard fried eggs.

Hal's father, his gray hair sticking out in all directions, shuffled down the hall. He plopped down at the table. Hal stared at the cholesterol, heart attack precursor filled plate Nora placed in front of her father. She made a mental note when her mother wasn't listening to remind him to go to the doctor for a physical once in awhile.

Jim winked at his wife and grinned at his daughter. "Well, how you feeling this morning, Hallie?"

"Not so hot," Hal conceded. She rubbed her stomach, feeling urpy now that she'd looked at and smelled his plate of food. She'd swear her mother deliberately waved it under her nose before she set the plate down.

"She's got wedding jitters," giggled Nora behind her hand to Jim.

"I have not. I'm just not hungry is all," snapped Hal, peevishly.

Jim shrugged his broad farmer shoulders. "Whatever you say, Daughter. But jitters are to be expected. If you was to have some, that is, it would be all right. By afternoon tomorrow

3

you'll be feeling less nervous once the wedding is over. What time is the wedding buggy coming for us in the morning?"

Hal's eyebrows furrowed together as she set her cup down. "There isn't any wedding buggy. What made you think there was?"

"Tootie told your mother her Amish book said you'd have to arrive at the wedding in a buggy," Jim said before he crunched on a bacon strip.

"That might be if you were Amish, but you're not and you don't own a buggy. For your information, we're going to the Lapp farm in your car in the morning. You're driving because you are my father," informed Hal.

"I thought you couldn't ride in a car after today," he said with a puzzled look.

"I can so ride in one. I'm just not supposed to drive one including my own," Hal groaned, tapping the table with her fingers.

Nora poured a cup of coffee and sit down next to Hal. She perked up as an idea struck her. "When you're ready to sell your car, Dear, can your cousin, Cindy, buy it? Tootie's been looking for a car for her to drive to college this fall."

"I'm not selling my car," Hal barked.

Jim looked baffled. "I thought you just said you couldn't drive it. You might as well get rid of it. Not good for a car to never be run."

"I'm stalling while I try to think of a way around that," retorted Hal, tipping the cup for the last sip. "Listen, I'm going to go take a shower and get ready to leave. Emma will be bustling around, trying to do everything by herself." She darted a look at her mother. "We might as well be useful *now that we're up*."

"Does it matter what I wear to the wedding?" Her father asked, looking worried.

"A suit would be nice," Hal explained patiently.

"I brought that. What do Amish men wear?"

"Black suits and black hats with a white shirt," she answered.

4

"They wear hats! I just bought a white western hat. I have it with me," Jim said excitedly.

"Oh, please no! Not a white western hat!" Hal cried.

"Why not?"

"The Amish wear black felt hats or straw hats, but during the wedding or a church meeting, they won't have a hat on. To wear a white hat wouldn't do at all at the wedding and maybe never when you're visiting the Amish," Hal scolded.

Jim scratched a sideburn. The action reminded Hal of John when he couldn't figure out what to make of her way of thinking. Finally, he said quietly, "All right, I won't wear the hat, but I still don't see why not."

"Because I want John and his children to like you. That's why not. Mom, can you explain it to him?" Hal pleaded.

Nora sighed and patted her hand. "I'll try, dear, but I'm confused, too. I'm not so sure I understand all this myself. It seems to me from what you tell us Amish life may be entirely different from the way Tootie drilled it into us."

Hal showered and put on her pale green dress and white apron. After she pulled a wet comb through her copper red hair, she braided as much of it as she could. She wrapped the braid around her head before she clamped her white prayer cap down tight. When she studied her image in the mirror, Hal gave herself a disgusted look. She had to face it. With bright, frizzy hair like hers, nothing was going to keep her from looking like Harpo Marx with a bald spot.

At the same time as she chided herself, she knew she should feel lucky. No matter how she looked, John and the kids seemed to love her anyway. She was getting a good, understanding Plain husband and a ready made family of three kids. Dear fifteen year old Emma was a mother hen to everyone including her. Frankly, Hal didn't know how she would manage being a housewife or motherhood if Emma wasn't there to help her. Being a nurse was a breeze compare to what Amish housewives had to know.

John's oldest son, Noah, twelve years old going on thirty, was so serious, and ten year old Daniel, kept excitement and fun in all their lives with his mischievous nature.

Hal grabbed the garbage sack stuffed with clothes out of the corner and headed for the living room. Mom watched out the window as a blue jay lit on the bird feeder. Her father had the local news channel on. Both of them seemed to be patiently waiting on her.

"Ready, you guys?" Hal asked.

"My don't you look -----," Nora searched for the right word as she surveyed her daughter.

"Different, Mom?" Hal questioned edgily. "Is that the word?"

"No, I wouldn't have said that at all. You look nice," Nora replied.

"Sorry it took me so long to get ready. I couldn't do a thing with my hair this morning," Hal complained.

"Why don't you get it cut off today," Jim suggested.

"Can't," Hal said quickly. "Amish women don't cut their hair ever."

Nora frowned, "Seems like there is an awful lot of don't rules when you belong to this group."

"Group? Mom, this isn't some club I'm joining. I'm getting married, and I'm part of the Amish faith now," Hal said plaintively.

"I agree with your mother. Can't you just tell them you forgot about rule 347 and go get your hair cut this once before they can stop you," her dad said dryly.

"No, I can't."

"Are there any good things about being Amish?" Nora asked, wrinkling up her nose.

"Yes, you're getting a nice son-in-law, three sweet grandchildren and a happy daughter," Hal assured her.

Putting a stop to the subject, Hal dropped the clothes bag and rushed back to her bedroom. She placed the box of pictures she'd forgotten earlier under her arm, letting it rest on her hip. Hal returned to the living room and handed her father the bag then ushered her parents out the door. She glanced back long enough to scan the living room and what she could see through

6

the door to the kitchen. John and the boys would help her move her things out of the apartment before the end of the month. The living room furniture was in better shape than John's so he was going to put those items in their living room. She was glad about that. The Lapp couch was in sad shape after all the years the children bounced on it.

Hal eyed the crystal stemmed lamp by her recliner. A breeze from the open door made the fringe on the end of the shade shutter. She liked that lamp, but it was electric. Not being able to keep that lamp meant good bye to one life and get used to another entirely different way of living. She hoped from tomorrow on her life would be all she wanted it to be, and that she'd prepared herself well enough to accept the drastic changes she faced.

Hal turned the key in the door lock and twisted around to find her mother watching her intently. "Are you sure, Hal, that this new life is really what you want?"

"I'm sure. I was just making a mental of list of my things that I could take to the farm." Hal sighed before she added, "I really like my crystal lamp, but it's electric. Suppose Cindy could use it in her college dorm?"

"Don't know, but if she doesn't want it I can find a place for the lamp," Nora said eagerly.

"All right, before you leave for home let's go for a walk through the apartment and anything with a cord that will fit in the car is yours," Hal said.

"You can change your mind," Nora suggested.

"No, I can't. This apartment is full of just stuff. I don't need stuff. I need John and the kids. I wouldn't back out on them. This new life is what I want, but sometimes I wonder if I'm up to the challenge of being Amish," Hal said.

"You can succeed at anything if you really want to. All you have to do is keep trying until you get it right," Nora said sagely.

"Is that all there is to it, Mom?"

"Being Amish is a new way of life for you. There are bound to be some mistakes made along the way, but your Amish family and friends will help you. Before you know it, you'll get the hang of it with John and the children by your side supporting you. I'm sure of it," Nora said, hugging her daughter.

The car window whine down. "Are you two coming? I won't get to the farm before John has the cows milked if you don't hurry."

An amber glow lit up the dark eastern sky as the top edge of the sun peeked above the apartment house across the street. Hal hated to say so out loud, but she feared her dad was right. The milking would be over before they got to the farm.

Chapter 2

Trees and buildings in countryside glowed red from the sunrise. An old weather saying came to Hal's mind. Red sky in the morning, sailor take warning. Not a good omen if she let herself believe in such old wives tales.

When they arrived at the Lapp farm at 5:30, the dark shadows of the farm buildings sprawled west into the driveway as the sun rose behind them. All was quiet in the barn, and the other helpers hadn't arrived yet.

When they got out of the car, Jim listened to the silence and groaned, "I told you if you two women didn't get a move on, I'd miss milking. That's just what happened."

"Cheer up, Dad. Maybe *John and the boys* were lucky enough to get to sleep in. If you did miss milking this time, chores happen twice a day. You'll get your share of milking until you're sick of it if you stick around," Hal assured him.

Nora teased, "Milking will make you remember why you sold the dairy cows."

Hal lead the way through the house and walked into the kitchen with her parents behind her. The sun shone through the open window and dappled the black and white linoleum, making the kitchen bright and cheery.

"Good morning, everyone," Hal greeted John and the children. They were eating breakfast.

John looked surprised. "Since your folks just got in last night, I didn't expect you this early."

"Mom's idea. Looks like my parents are eager to get me married off," Hal quipped.

"Hallie Lindstrom, what a thing to say," Nora chided,

blushing when John smiled at her.

The prospective bridegroom stood up and motioned for his children to join him.

Hal introduced, "John, this is my parents, Nora and Jim."

John shook Nora's hand. "Wie bist du beit, Nora."

Nora looked at Hal for a translation. "He says it's nice to meet you."

As Jim shook hands with John, Hal finished with, "These are John's children. Emma, Noah and Daniel."

Jim shook hands with each of them. "We bust do bet, you all." The kids snickered behind their hands. "Was I even close?" Jim asked, grinning at them.

Emma laughed. "With some practice, you will be speaking Deutsche before you know it."

Nora, on the other hand, gave each of the kids a big hug. "It's nice to finally meet my new grandchildren and son-in-law." She smiled at the kids warmly.

Emma ducked her head bashfully. "Sit down please and have a cup of coffee. We will be running ourselves ragged to get everything done later. Have you had breakfast?"

"Yes, Dear, so you go ahead and finish eating before your food gets cold. Anyway, Jim did. I wasn't hungry, and Hal has the wedding jitters. She wouldn't eat," Nora shared.

"Mom, for Pete sakes," Hal groaned as John winked at her. The look on his face told her she was in for more teasing from him if Mom kept going.

"I guess you already milked," Jim quizzed John.

"Just finished. We were up and at 'em early this morning," John replied.

Nora brightened. "That reminds me. What time do you usually get -----."

"Mom!" Interrupted Hal shrilly. Everyone stared at her. She tried to breathe in easy and sound quietly calm when she said, "Mom, Emma is getting your coffee. Why don't you sit down at the table and drink it. Emma, I think I'd like a cup, too."

Very softly, Nora muttered to no one in particular, "We should shut you off. I think you've had enough coffee already."

None of them acknowledged they heard Nora, but Jim's mouth twitched at the corners as he spoke to Jim. "Can you stay a few days after the wedding so we can get acquainted? We have a spare bedroom that is yours as long as you want it."

"We'd like that. I'm thinking my farm can get along without me for a few days," Jim said. When he saw John lift an eyebrow, he added, "I gave up livestock some time back. All I have now is crop ground. Harvest is a few weeks off yet."

"Besides, we'd like to get to know Hal's family a little better. We live so far apart," Nora said regretfully. Emma sat down by Nora and received another hug. "Listen, if you ever feel comfortable with doing it, I'd love to be called Grandma." She looked accusingly at Hal, laying the blame on her. "Seems like I've waited forever to hear someone call me that."

Emma smiled at her. "Jah, to call you Mammi Nora des gute."

"Hey, how about me? I'm Grandpa," Jim said, pointing to himself. Then he ruffled the hair on the boys heads, sitting on either side of him. They didn't speak, but Hal could tell they were sizing up this stranger. She just hoped her English father wasn't so forward that he scared the timid boys away. It was easy to do. She remembered her first encounter with them. Her sharp tongue had sent both boys scurrying from the room like startled rabbits when she was John's home health nurse.

"Jah, you are for sure our Dawdi Jim." Emma laughed as Jim gave her a wink.

Hal was proud of her parents at that moment. They had won Emma over. One down and two kids to go.

"Sounds like you just made it here before the rest of our help arrived. Listen," Emma said, heading out of the kitchen to the front door. The crunch of buggy wheels on gravel was loud, coming through the open kitchen window.

Hal peeked past the curtain at a dozen buggies coming from both directions. They slowed down to take their turn coming into the driveway. "Would you look at this? Mom and Dad, it's the Amish version of rush hour traffic."

As people filed up on the front porch, Hal introduced them

to her parents. Emma directed women to the kitchen, and John took charge of the men.

Emma introduced Roseanna and Samuel Nisely to Hal's parents.

"Believe I'll go with the men otherwise the women might have me washing dishes or something else equally disagreeable. Mind if I tag along, Samuel?" Jim asked.

Ducking his head, Samuel chuckled. "Komm quickly with me."

Next in line was Luke Yoder, his wife, Linda, and his mother, Margaret. The four Yoder children, Levi, Jennie, Mark and Rose, tagged along back of their parents and grandmother. Behind them was a young man Hal didn't know. Hal hugged both women before she introduced them to her mother and then introduced the rest of the family. She told Luke to find John, He would be giving instructions to the men. The biggest chore was to help pitch the tent before the bench wagons arrived.

"Daed, we should get busy." Seventeen year old Levi, a fair young man like his father, started to leave, but he noticed Hal and Emma staring at the stranger, a gangly young man. "This is Josh Beiler. He is staying with us while he works for Daed."

The young man took his straw hat off to reveal a shock of unruly black hair. He nodded at Hal, staring listlessly at her from under his averted head. When his attention turned to Emma, he livened up as he inspected the girl from her head to the hem of her skirt.

Hal didn't like the curious gleam in his dark eyes. She was relieved to find the girl's attention was directed toward the women. She ushered them toward the kitchen and completely missed Josh's inspection.

By the middle of the morning, the driveway was filled with buggies. In the grassy lawn beside the clinic, men pitched the large tent. The two bench wagons arrived before lunch time. The drivers parked near the barn and hopped down, strolling toward the tent. The church district's one wagon of benches wouldn't be enough so wagon number two was sent for from another district. The tent was almost secured. Next, the men needed to unloaded the benches and carry them inside the tent. The legs were unfolded, and the benches arranged for the congregation.

While the men finished putting up the tent, John came in the mud room and stood in the kitchen doorway. Jim was right behind him.

Emma pointed to the two steaming pails on the wood cookstove. "Daed, the water is hot enough to scald the chickens. You ready to butcher? Cutting the chicken's heads off and cleaning them will take awhile."

Jim asked from behind John, "How many chickens you plan on butchering?"

John turned to him. "Forty fryers should feed everyone for the wedding lunch."

Jim snorted, "Is that all. Maybe I better tag along and help."

"Not in those good clothes, you're not," admonished Nora. "I'd hate to see how you looked later with all that blood and feathers on you. What will all these people think of you for the rest of the day?"

John suggested, "Mind wearing some of my chore clothes until we get done?"

"Not at all. Get them for me," Jim said eagerly.

When the men came back downstairs and went out the back door, Hal grinned at how Amish her father looked except he was minus a beard. She peeked out the door later. Several headless fryers spurted blood as they flopped this way and that in the grass around the gathered men.

Emma said, looking over Hal's shoulder, "That group of men are witnesses to how good a job Daed does chopping off the heads. He needs to kill every chicken with one chop. Some people still believe he will have bad luck of some kind if he does not."

John held a rooster by the legs and raised the hatchet up high. He came down hard. The hatchet went through the rooster's neck with a resounding thud and cut into the wood block. The rooster's body struggled in John's hand until he let go. The chicken somersaulted in a circle and headed toward the

13

men. They scattered. Somehow, the headless rooster got to his feet and made a stiff legged hop a couple of times then flopped over on his side, kicking. By that time, the chicken left blood from John's farmer shoes across the grass. A crimson trail that crisscrossed all the other headless roosters bloody paths.

Emma said to Hal, "I think it's time the witnesses willfully partaken picking feathers." She went after the water to scald the fryers.

Hal heard one of the men say to Jim, "Do you have as much wind up north as we do here?"

She froze in her tracks, waiting to see how her father answered.

"It's bad up our way all right. Wind gets so strong. Sometimes when the hens lay their eggs, the wind blows the eggs right back into where they came out of," Jim allowed.

"Oh Dad," Hal groaned to herself. She bent her head into the door facing to hide her face and waited for the farmer's reaction.

All the men looked at each other and at Jim. He grinned from ear to ear, and they burst out laughing. Hal blew out a breath. It might take awhile but just maybe these Plain farmers would get the hang of her father's sense of humor.

"What was so funny?" Emma asked as she came out the door with a potholder around the hot handle of a pail.

"You don't want to know," Hal declared softly. "Trust me."

Emma sat the steaming water down near the men. She informed them they could dunk the chickens and start picking as her father killed the rest. She pointed to a metal grain basket nearby to put the feathers in.

When Emma came back by her, Hal asked, "What happens to the chickens after they're cleaned?"

"Four ladies will take them home to roast tonight so the meat will be ready by lunch time tomorrow. Now I've got one more bucket of water to bring out. Come with me and get the dish pans to lay the chickens in after they are picked."

Emma returned with the bucket and placed it in front of the men. One man was dunking a fryer up and down in the other steaming pail. Hal put the dish pans on the ground close by.

Emma said to her, "We better keep at it in the kitchen." The girl took Hal by the elbow and headed for the house. Once they were inside, she pointed to the table. "You have potatoes to peel."

Hal gasped at the mountain of potatoes piled on the table beside a large kettle and a paring knife. "That many?"

"Jah, this is going to be a big wedding. We have a lot of people to feed," Emma assured her. "Everyone has a job today. Some are cooking for today's meal and some for tomorrow. Look, Roseanna Nisely is making doughnuts for the wedding."

"Oh good! Roseanna, your doughnuts are the best," Hal complimented.

Roseanna blushed as she put flour in a big mixing bowl. She wasn't used to a compliment that caused her to be the center of attention.

"Three women have been assigned to bake cookies this afternoon for tomorrow. Margaret Yoder has already brought a large batch of oatmeal cookies for today," Emma said.

"How about I help you peel potatoes?" Margaret offered softly in Hal's ear. She adjusted her cap over her silver threaded dark hair as she looked in the utensil drawer for a paring knife.

"That would be great. As slow as I peel I could use the help," Hal whispered behind her hand.

Serious Emma ignored their banter. "Edna Esch is bringing peanut butter cookies. Jane Bontrager is baking sugar cookies and ----." She paused to wiped a wrinkle out of her apron. Then she said very quietly, "Stella Strutt has offered to bring molasses ones."

Hal glanced around to see if anyone was listening. She said pointedly, "Stella Strutt's coming to help?"

Emma nodded. "It wouldn't be right to not ask her. She is a member of this church district. If she wants to help, it would not be right to leave her out, would it?"

"No, I guess not," Hal agreed reluctantly.

Emma put her hand on Hal's arm and said softly just for

Hal's ears, "You must act kindly toward her. That is our way."

Hal smiled wryly. "I get it. I need to turn the other cheek."

"Jah," Emma agreed smiling back. "You have it right now."

Hal sat down and picked up the paring knife. Margaret gave her a warm smile that lit her hazel eyes as she scooted her chair close. She reached past Hal for a potato. "So have you got wedding day jitters yet?"

"I didn't think so but my parents seem to think I have," Hal related, nodding at her mother.

A low vibrating rumble came from her skirt pocket. Hal darted a sheepish glance around her. Thank goodness. With so much talking and kitchen noises, the other women didn't hear the buzz. How could she have forgotten to turn the ringer off on her cell phone? To make matters worse, it was vibrating against Margaret's thigh.

When she felt the vibration, the wrinkles fanned out at the corners of the older woman's eyes as she tried to stifle a giggle and choked. "Is that a bee hive in your pocket by chance?" She patted her chest as she whispered.

Hal looked worried. "No, my phone. You aren't going to tell on me, are you?"

Margaret glanced over her shoulder. "No need to if it keeps ringing. Let these women quiet down a minute, and they will hear for themselves," she predicted.

"I'll be right back." Hal rushed from the kitchen, headed for the privacy of the clinic. In the living room, she tried to walk calmly past John's sister, Amy, busy knocking cobwebs out of the corner with the broom. The woman, so intent on reaching as high as she could, didn't hear Hal glide behind her.

After Hal closed the clinic door, she answered the phone in a whisper. "Hello."

"It's Barb Sloan. Why are you whispering?"

"I have a whole kitchen full of Amish women cooking and one in the living room doing broom combat with the spiders."

"And you're whispering because ----?"

Hal confided, "Because I'm not supposed to have a phone anymore. I don't think. Now I'm alone in the clinic with the door closed so we can talk."

Barb gave an audible gasp on the other end of the line. "You don't know if you can have a phone? Why don't you ask?"

"Oh sure! Calling attention to the phone is a sure fire way to get it taken away from me. I think I'll just keep still thank you very much," retorted Hal, mildly defensive.

Barb asked, "How's everything going? You sound edgy. Did your parents get here all right?"

"They came in yesterday afternoon and are driving me up a wall already," Hal admitted frankly.

Barb giggled. "Oh, it can't be that bad."

"Want to bet. They were afraid I'd wind up an old maid. Now they're thrilled to be marrying me off and going overboard with this whole getting to know everyone thing." Hal heard the uncontrolled laughter on the other end. She wanted to yell at her friend but she resisted. John's sister might hear her and come after her with the broom. How would that look the day before the wedding if John's family decided he was marrying a lunatic?

"What I called for was to ask if you needed help. I can come out and pitch in this morning," Barb said.

"I'd love it. Maybe you can help me keep an eye on my parents so they don't get me excommunicated before I get married," Hal pleaded.

Barb choked on a giggle. "You're not serious."

Hal tried to keep the desperation out of her voice. "Seems Mom's sister brainwashed my parents with all kinds of myths she found in a library book on the Amish. No telling what's going to come out of my parents mouth thanks to Aunt Tootie."

Barb smothered her laughter. "All right, I'm on my way."

Quietly, Hal edged behind Amy and back into the kitchen. When she sat down, Margaret gave her a light poke with her elbow and whispered, "Get rid of the bees?"

"I hid the bees in the clinic, and it shall stay there," Hal vowed.

Margaret leaned over to drop a potato in the kettle. With a dubious look, she said, "Gute."

Chapter 3

Hoping that Margaret would not get her in trouble about the phone, Hal picked up her knife and quietly worked on a potato. While she peeled, Hal glanced around her at the women working so hard to make her wedding day special. Roseanna and Nora stood close together at one end of the counter. Roseanna kneaded her doughnut dough on the floured surface as she asked Nora where she lived. Nora cut celery into serving sizes for relish plates as she answered.

Emma had friends her age, Mary Ruth and Ida Janzen, helping her make sandwiches for lunch. Jennie Yoder was washing dishes right next to them. The girls were discussing where and when the next Sunday evening singing was to be held. With intermittent low giggles, the girls talked, as most young girls would, about boys and which teenagers might come as a couple.

At the other end of the counter, Lizzy Leichenring hit boiled eggs, one at a time, against the hard surface then picked off the shells. The quiet woman made more noise with those eggs then Hal had heard from her in all the time she'd known Lizzy.

Hal saw Amy dart by the doorway. She was sweeping every nook and cranny with the intention of dusting when she was done. Hal wondered if this was just busy work on Amy's part. After all, Emma or Hal took a turn sweeping every morning. The house couldn't be that dirty.

John's other sister, Beth, was outside on a stepladder washing windows. Hal had to admit the windows needed cleaning. All the dust from the traffic on the gravel road settled on the glass, making a filmy haze which had been hard to see through. She hoped she had time to visit with both her new sister-in-laws later. She wanted to get to know John's family as soon as possible.

About a half hour later, Barb yelled as she crossed the living room, "Anyone home?"

Amy rested on the broom handle and answered, "Jah, they are in the kitchen."

Hal went to greet her friend at the doorway. "Very funny. Everyone, this is my friend Barb Sloan. She volunteered to help us."

"Wilcom, Barb Sloan. Can you make potato salad?" Emma asked with directness.

"Yes, I'm quite good at it as a matter of fact," Barb bragged rolling up her blouse sleeves.

"Gute. You can help make some for today's lunch. Start chopping up that bowl of cold potatoes while Lizzy chops the eggs. You'll find onion and mayonnaise beside the bowl. If you need anything else just ask," Emma instructed. She looked out the kitchen window. "Oh, oh, here comes, Stella Strutt."

Hal asked half heartedly, "You want me to go greet her since I'm already up?"

"Nah, you continue peeling. I will see to Stella," Emma said as she dashed past Hal.

As Hal sat down, she heard the girl greet, "Wilcom, Stella Strutt. How are you this day?"

"Not a bit well, a bit well atall," the older woman said in her loud, quarrelsome voice. "I decided to bring these cookies over now. Best get them here while they are fresh, real fresh."

"Denke for helping us. Come in the kitchen with the other women," invited Emma.

"Nah, I'm going back home, back home. When it is hot like today, my ankles swell. Really swelled today. See." The elderly woman must have paused to lift her long black dress enough to expose her puffy ankles and feet. Her swelled legs stretched her black socks, and her feet spilled over her sensible black shoes. "I need to get off my feet this afternoon so I will feel like coming to the wedding tomorrow," Stella explained in stilted dialect.

"I am sorry to hear that," Emma said sympathetically.

Hal giggled as she listened to the strained silence in the living room. Stella didn't speak but Hal could imagine the caustic look she gave Emma.

Apologetically, Emma said, "Ach nah, Stella! I did not mean I was sorry you are coming to the wedding. I meant I am sorry to hear you are not well."

"I see. I see." Stella mumbled as she walked heavy footed to the door and shut it with a bang.

Margaret, with a twinkle in her eyes, elbowed Hal and scolded, "Pay attention to your job, Hal. We will never get the kettle full if you keep whittling your potatoes down to the size of pullet eggs."

"I'm sorry," Hal said meekly, tossing the much smaller potato in the pot. She knew it was not the Amish way to gloat, but she was suddenly very glad Emma chose to deal with Stella Strutt.

Lizzy finished chopping the last egg in the bowl and washed her hands. She disappeared into the mud room. When she came back she was carrying a pail of water and a broom.

Emma asked, "What are you going to do, Lizzy?"

"When I came this morning, I noticed where chickens had roosted on the edge of your porch. I have the eggs ready for the salad so I thought I'd clean the porch. If that is all right with you?" Lizzy suggested hesitantly.

"That is an every day job, but the mess is from the ducks that follow the hen they think is their mother onto the porch. I've been meaning to talk to my brothers about doing something with those ducks. I will not have time to clean the porch off in the morning. I have a notion the porch floor will look the same way tomorrow as it does every morning," complained Emma.

She headed for the front door with Lizzy following her. "Noah and Daniel," she shouted. The boys looked toward the house. She beckoned them to come. When they were close, Emma said, "I want you to catch those little ducks and take them to the pond. They are big enough to take care of themselves. We do not want this mess on the porch in the morning," she said, pointing to the smeared brown and white splashes dotting the board floor.

"All right," Noah said. He took off around the house with Daniel chasing after him. They peeked in the hen house and searched around the yard. Behind the building, a molting red hen, dressed in one tail feather and a few ragged wing feathers, was working to cover four good sized mallards that insisted on bulldozing their way under her wings.

The boys edged along the building. When they were close enough, they dived onto the squawking hen and held her down while they felt under her wings for duck legs.

Once they had the very vocal quackers caught, the boys headed for the pond. They walked down to the bank, holding the dangling ducks.

Noah planned, "I think we should set the ducks loose in different places so they are not together. You go around the pond aways and turn your two loose in different places. I will go around this way and end up on the dam."

Daniel waded the knee high weeds along the edge of the bank. He stopped at a spot the cows had tromped down to get a drink. The bank slanted, making it easy to get to the water. Squatting, the boy sat a duck on his webbed feet. The duck quacked loudly, waddled out of Daniel's reach and slid off the bank into the water. The half grown mallard glided to the middle of the pond and met up with Noah's two ducks. Daniel thought for a minute. He didn't see how turning the ducks loose in different spots had helped keep them separated. They joined back up in the pond. He let go of the other duck and watched him swim to the others.

Ready to go back to the house, Daniel kicked his way through the marshy grass. A startled frog crocked a loud protest when the boy came too close. Daniel jumped sideways. The boy's quick movement caused the frog to leap high in the air. He plunked down in the tall grass a few feet ahead of the boy and hunkered down. Keeping his eyes on where the frog lit, Daniel edged up to him and pounced. He missed. The frog

21

jumped out of reach just in time but the wrong way. Daniel edged between the frog and the pond. This time, the frog leaped a few feet ahead and crept under a patch of beaten down marsh grass to hide. Daniel saw his chance. He quietly eased up to the frog. Slowly, he bent over with his hands out. The frog saw him coming. He struggled to keep moving but found himself caught in the tangled grass. The frog thrashed about, kicking with his strong legs until Daniel's hands eased around him with a strong grip.

What a beauty! This is one of the largest frogs I have ever seen. He is going to make a great pet. What should I name him? A frog this large should have a name to match. He is a giant among frogs. Daniel toed a clump of grass as he thought. *Goliath! That name will do.* Daniel searched the pasture. Noah was almost back to the barn. He stuffed the struggling frog into his pocket and sprinted as fast as he could after his brother. His mind was on where he should keep his new pet.

Late that afternoon, the men joined the others in the living room. Delighted to be able to help with the milking, Jim told Nora, "That was fun. I didn't realize how much I missed milking cows."

"I'm glad you enjoyed yourself, Dear," Nora said, patting his knee.

Noah smiled at his new grandfather's enthusiasm, "Dawdi, you are wilcom to come help us do the milking any time you want."

"If you like chores, you can help me feed the pigs in the morning," Daniel piped up.

"While you are at it, boys, why not give Jim a list of all our chores. He can have fun doing them all while we rest in the house," John teased.

"Ach, Daed!" Noah said, ducking his head.

Jim laughed then stifled a yawn. Hal could see from the looks on their faces, her parents were tired. Soon one or both of them would be nodding off. "Mom and Dad, I think it's time we went back to the apartment."

"You are wilcom to stay for supper before you go," Emma

invited.

"Not this time. If we think today was exhausting, wait until tomorrow," Hal predicted.

"Sounds like a good idea to get back to Wickenburg while we're still awake. We do need to get to bed early tonight," Nora agreed.

As her parents went down the porch steps, John grabbed Hal by the elbow. "You can spend the night if you want to rather than drive back to town."

Hal whispered to him, "Not unless you want to bunk with my father and me with my mother. The English, in my parents generation, wouldn't want to see us share a bed tonight."

"Have you tried to explain bundling to them so you could sleep in my bed tonight?"

"No, because they wouldn't believe putting pillows between me and you would work. They would be right. From what I remember of the night you suggested it, bundling failed," Hal said, tugging gently on John's beard. "See you bright and early in the morning."

Once they hit the Wickenburg city limits, Hal suggested, "How about we stop somewhere to eat supper? No fuss, no mess. Besides, my cupboards are about bare. Didn't see any sense in stocking up again."

"All right with us. We don't need a very big supper after all that good food Emma fed us for lunch," Nora said.

"Alperson's Maid Rite is a great place to get a sandwich and fries," Hal told them as she pulled into the diner parking lot.

Middle aged Millie Alperson, the blond, blue eyed owner and waitress, waved from behind the counter. She gave Hal's Amish clothing an up and down once over as she slowly said, "Hi, Hal. Haven't seen you for a while obviously."

"Been busy. I'm getting married tomorrow," Hal offered.

"Well, congratulations. Who's the lucky fellow?"

"John Lapp."

Millie, who thought she knew everyone in town, puzzled over the name a moment. "Oh yeah, that's one of the Amish farmers out southwest of town."

"You got it. Millie, meet my mother and father, Nora and Jim Lindstrom from Titonka, Iowa. They're here for the wedding. We need a quick supper. I told them you had the best Maid Rites ever," Hal stated.

Millie beamed with pride. "Nice to meet you folks. Thanks for the compliment, Hal. We aim to please. Give me your orders and take a seat at that corner table. I'll serve you."

Hal plopped down and leaned back in her chair. She yawned. "Maybe sitting down isn't too good an idea. I'll hate to get up from here to go to the car when my stomach is full."

She noticed her mother staring over her shoulder, but it was too late to duck out of sight when she heard the familiar, smooth male voice. "Hello Hal."

Dreading the person she'd see, Hal twisted in her seat. "Hello. Phil King, meet my parents, Jim and Nora Lindstrom."

"So nice to meet you folks." Phil pulled up a chair from an empty table and sat down.

He hasn't changed one bit. Thinks he can butt in and just make himself at home without being invited, Hal thought.

"Been awhile since I've seen you, Hallie. How you been?" Phil sounded genuinely interested as he absentmindedly rubbed his chest in a circle motion. Hal wondered if looking at her gave him phantom pains where she hit him with the skillet the last time she saw him.

"I'm fine. Been busy. Visiting with my parents as you can see," Hal said shortly.

Phil studied her clothes intently. "Looks like you're going Amish on me or is that a costume for a masquerade party I didn't know about." Under his breath, he said, "I can only hope."

"I am Amish," Hal said curtly. "Now if you will excuse us. We'd like to eat our supper. Millie's coming with our food."

Phil's amazed face showed he couldn't quite grasp the idea of an Amish Hallie Lindstrom. He said with meaning as he concentrated on her face, "I want you to know you're in my thoughts more than I care to admit."

"Don't admit it then. As a matter of fact, I don't want you to

24

think about me at all, Phil. I've moved on. You should, too," Hal said curtly. She was afraid to look in her parents direction. She could imagine how very attentive the two of them were to this whole mess of a conversation. The one thing she didn't intend to explain to them later was Phil King.

Phil wiggled a pointed finger in the air up and down from her prayer cap to her dress. "Is this a for sure done deal?"

"Yes, it's a very done deal, and I'm not changing my mind. Good bye, Phil," Hal said curtly. Millie placed a black plastic woven platter in front of her. Hal concentrated on opening the wrapper on a maid rite to avoided Phil's eyes and her parents curious stares.

As Millie served Hal's parents, Phil rose slowly. He studied Hal with sad eyes. "I'm sorry to hear that. Hope you folks have a good visit with Hal," Phil said, nodding politely at her parents.

As Nora watched the man walk away, she leaned toward Hal and whispered, "I don't recall you ever mentioning Mr. King before."

"Not much to mention where he's concerned," Hal said offhandedly.

"Don't seem like he sees it that way," Jim said, watching Phil as he left the cafe.

"What he thinks and sees doesn't matter to me," Hal said testily. "Now eat up you two so we can get to bed."

Chapter 4

The Lapp family sat around the kitchen table, finishing up breakfast. The early morning sun let a streak of bright sunlight shine over the half white curtain on the window.

Emma glanced at the clock above the sink and suggested, "I think we better get our wedding clothes on. People will be arriving soon."

"You're right, dear. Eight thirty will be here before we know it," Nora agreed. "Jim and I dressed for this occasion at the apartment so we're good to go."

John, Hal, Emma and the boys went upstairs. When Hal came back down, she was dressed in the light blue dress, white apron and a white cape she'd sewed for the wedding. Emma was in pink.

Jim puzzled, "Where's your wedding gown, Hallie?"

"Jim, Tootie says Amish brides wear blue," Nora told him.

"Sure don't look like it cost very much. Guess a dress like that isn't going to be hard for me to pay for," Jim said.

"It's all right, Dad. I paid for the material for the bridal dress and the attendant dresses," Hal told him."You see, we had to sew our dresses ourselves. Emma helped me with mine."

"No, kidding." Jim sounded impressed as he check out Emma's dress, too. "Guess I'm off the hook for this wedding, huh?"

"Actually, Tootie says the Amish book says the father of the bride pays for the whole Amish wedding," Nora informed him.

"All right, Hal, just let me know -----," Jim started.

"Relax, Dad. We aren't a young couple just starting out. John and I have this covered," Hal said, kissing her father on the

26

cheek.

"And we have a good day to have a wedding on," Nora stated. "Reminds me of a saying I've heard from Tootie. When the sun shines, happy will be the bride."

Hal giggled as she hugged her mother. "Now there's one thing I agree with Aunt Tootie on, but I'll be happy even if it was pouring down rain just in case she ever asks you."

Emma had only been half listening as she inspected her brothers. "Noah and Daniel, are you completely ready?"

They nodded. Noah said, "We will go outside out of the way." They raced across the living room before Emma could think of anything they might have forgotten to do. Daniel was last one out the door. He batted the screen door with his hands, let it sway wide open and slam shut. Emma and Hal flinched.

Emma ran to the door. "Daniel, come right back here."

The boy shuffled up the porch steps. "What is it?"

"You have to quit slamming this door. You're going to make Hallie and me old before our time. Now come back in here and close the door three times gently so you remember," Emma bossed.

Daniel gave his sister a suffering look and watched over his shoulder as she disappeared into the kitchen. He took hold of the door and counted as he opened the door a crack and shut it quickly. "One, two, three." He rushed out the door, letting it slam and ran after Noah.

From the kitchen window, Emma scolded, "Daniel!"

As the boys strolled across the yard, Levi Yoder called, "Come here, Noah." Levi was one of the boys chosen to be a wedding hostler so he'd made sure to be there early. Leaning against the barn beside him was the Yoders gangly hired hand.

Daniel heard Levi say to Noah, "Meet Josh Beiler. He's working for my daed now."

Noah gave Josh a good once over. He didn't like the sharp, arrogant look he got in return. He replied simply, "I know. I remember him coming to help yesterday."

On his own mission, Daniel kept going. He walked around the side of the barn to the attached lean to. He got down on his

27

knees between the buggy and the carriage. The bulge in his trouser pocket on the right wiggled. The boy reached in and pulled out the bull frog. "Was ist letz? You want a little fresh air?"

The frog struggled in Daniel's tight grip. "All right, I will put you down for a moment, Goliath." He sat the frog on the ground but he held onto the wiggling creature's back legs. It had been hard enough to catch the frog the first time. Daniel didn't want to have to chase Goliath down again right now. He didn't have time. The wedding would start soon.

From in front of the barn, Noah called, "Daniel, where you at?"

"Beside the barn." He stood up, stuffed Goliath back in his pocket and wiped his hands on his trouser legs.

When Noah got to him, he shook his head at Daniel critically. "Look at your trouser knees. All dirty and the wedding is about to start. We need to get in line."

Noah walked away leaving Daniel to dust his knees for a second. Though his trouser legs weren't quite perfect, he stopped when he felt he looked good enough to suit himself. He ran after Noah to get into the greeting line.

The wedding party was assembled on a bench in front of the tent. John was between his two witnesses, Samuel Nisely and Henry Lapp, a cousin of John's. Hal sat between her two witnesses, Emma and Margaret Yoder while they greeted the guests.

The forgehers (ushers) escorted the ministers in first to chairs that faced the wedding guests and the bridal party chairs. After the well wishers passed by the wedding party, they gathered to the side in groups to wait their turn to be taken into the tent by the ushers. After the ministers had been seated first, the relatives of the bride and groom went inside.

Guests were seated by age and relationship to the bride and groom. A task made easy at this wedding by the fact that Hal's only invited friend was Barb Sloan and her only relatives were her parents. So Barb would get a front row seat on the women's side. Women sat on the left and men on the right. Young relatives came in next so the ushers motioned for Noah and Daniel to come with them. Next were the couples recently married or had published their intention in church to marry. They came in together then separated to their respective sections. Cousins and friends concluded the procession of young people. A couple empty benches were left at the very back for the helpers to sit on when they had a moment to get away from the kitchen.

All the men had left their hats on the shelves in the bench wagons. Removal of hats signified that the tent was now a place of worship. This fine morning, the better portion of the district's congregation was gathered together and ready to witness this wedding. The ministers kept their hats on until the first song was over which was according to an old custom.

Levi Yoder and several other hostlers saw to it that the teams were unhitched from carriages parked in the hayfield. The two lines of enclosed carriages stretched the width of the hayfield. The horses were tied to a rope stretched between two tractors with steel wheels. This rope was in the middle between the two lines of buggies. When the families were ready to leave, the men had to know which horses and carriages belonged to them. They had to hitch their own horses up.

In the driveway, cars, pickups and vans, belonging to English and Mennonites, parked nosed toward the yard with the front wheels on the grass. In the midst of the vehicles was Barb's blue convertible with the top down.

Promptly at eight thirty, Bishop Elton Bontrager, Minister Luke Yoder and Deacon Enos Yutzy, sat down in chairs facing the congregation filing in with the ushers. Bishop Bontrager called for the ushers to tell the wedding party to come in and take their seats in the row of chairs that faced the ministers. The attendants paired off. Samuel Nisely took Emma's hand, and they walked down the aisle. John and Hal, holding hands, walked to their seats. Henry and Margaret followed. In the seating arrangement as when they greeted the guests, John and Hal sat between their two attendants.

Bishop Bontrager, a short, heavy set man with a red

29

complexion, stood and announced the opening of the wedding service. "Bruders and Schwesterns, we are ready to begin this wedding. Joe Miller, will you lead the first hymn."

The tall, thin song leader stood up and announced the hymn number from the Ausbund. Pages rustled as people rifled through their hymn books, locating the song. Once the page had been found the inside of the tent was so silent, Hal thought she'd be able to hear a pen drop if any of the women lost one. Joe Miller began the song in a loud clear voice and the rest joined in.

On the third line of the song, Bishop Bontrager, Minister Yoder and Deacon Yutzy rose to their feet and walk down the aisle and out of the tent. John took Hal by the elbow and helped her stand. They followed the ministers. The group headed for the two benches facing each other under the shade tree. John and Hal sat on one bench, and the ministers the other.

The hymn ended. One of the men started to sing the Lob Lied song. *O Gott Vater Wir Loben Dich*. The clear tenor voice projected the words, and everyone joined in. Hal was glad that she could understand the song's words now - Oh Father God, we praise Thee. When Emma told her, they sang a song with long verses that lasted close to five minutes each, Hal had been curious about the song. She could now see it would take that long when the verses were sang so slow. She looked at John and then at the ministers somber faces. Now wasn't the time to concentrate on that song or any other. She came to sit under the shade tree with John in front of the ministers for a reason. This was part of their wedding ceremony.

Bishop Bontrager cleared his throat and began his counseling. "You are taking a serious step this day to become man and wife, John Lapp and Hallie Lindstrom. I take it you must have given this much thought for some time."

John and Hal nodded in agreement.

Luke Yoder, minister and their friend, turned his attention on Hal. His friendly, easy going demeanor she'd seen so often was gone. He had turned serious. His clear blue eyes seemed to probe deeply into her soul as he explained, "It has been told to you that no divorce is allowed. Once you marry John Lapp it will be for life. Do you agree to this commitment for the rest of your life, Hallie Lindstrom?"

"I do," Hal said quietly.

The Bishop looked from John to Hal and back to John. "Are you ready and willing to marry this woman today?"

"I am," John stated with determination.

The bishop focused on Hal. "Hallie Lindstrom, are you ready and willing to marry this man this day?"

"I am," she replied.

The bishop bowed his head and blessed the couple with a prayer. When he was done, the ministers stood up.

"Gute. Go into the tent. We will be in shortly to get the ceremony started," Luke said, shaking hands with them.

Hallie licked her lips and said, "There is one thing I'd like to ask."

Bishop Bontrager's eyebrows shot up as he asked, "What?"

"Would it be permissible to speak much of the service in English so that my parents will be able to understand the ceremony." Hal looked from Elton to Luke. "You see, I'm their only child. I'd like them to be able to understand the wedding."

Elton studied his hands clasped in front of him. He raised his head and smiled at Hallie, "I think in this case, that would be a gute thing."

"Denke," Hal said.

After the couple's dismissal, the ministers had to take the time to decide among themselves who would take the different parts of the wedding ceremony. While they did that, John and Hal walked back down the aisle to take their seats between the wedding attendants.

After John and Hal sat down, the "Wedding Hymn" began, lead by Samuel Nisely in his full throated voice.

This song was the ministers cue that their time was up. They reentered the tent and took their places. Bishop Bontrager sat down the middle chair between the other two, and they joined in the singing.

After that song was over, Luke Yoder stood, tall and straight,

31

as he gave his sermon. He smiled down at Hallie's mother as he said, "We are going to use English for the sermons and scripture reading this day so that the bride's parents will be able to understand what is said."

He began with, "It says in the bible that Jesus prayed for those who crucified him. He cried, 'Father, forgive them for they know not what they do.'

Can we really figure out why God sent this or that to happen? Not really. It is not our place to judge. God is the great one. Circumstances sometimes test our faith, but our faith should never be shaken. This is something we have to continually work on."

After he ended his sermon, Minster Yoder bowed his head. "Let us have a silent prayer. All will kneel."

The congregation stood up, turned around and knelt, leaning over their benches. When the prayer was over, the congregation stood, but they didn't turn around.

Deacon Enos Yutzy stood up and moved forward to read scripture. "The Kingdom of Heaven is like to a grain of mustard seed which a man took and sowed in his field. Which indeed is the least of all seeds, but when it is grown, it is the greatest among herbs, and becometh a tree so that the birds of the air come and lodge in the branches."

When Deacon Yutzy finished reading, the congregation turned around and sat down. As the deacon sat down, Bishop Bontrager stood up to give his message. "We all must remember the husband has the major responsibility of directing the home for the glory of Christ. He needs to have the proper relationship with Christ in submission and self denial to glorify his Head. His is the God delegated authority over the woman and is responsible for her actions in the home and in society.

Husbands love your wives, even as Christ also loved the church, and gave himself for it. For this cause, a man shall be joined unto his wife, and they shall be one flesh as was Isaac to Rebekah." This well spoken man long ago had memorized many of the passages he used in his sermons so story telling came easy to him.

32

"In all the wedding ceremonies that I've told the story of Rebekah and Isaac wedding from the book of Genesis, I do not remember ever having a bride that was more like Rebekah than Hallie Lindstrom is. Hallie has given up one way of life to enter another so that she can wed John Lapp. Maybe there is no one that can know how great Hallie's sacrifice has been other than God.

Now I will speak of Rebekah who was willing to please God in any way she could. She lived 500 miles away from Isaac in Haran. It says in the bible, Abraham wanted a bride for his son, Isaac, but not a woman that lived nearby. The people in Canaan did not worship God.

Abraham sent his servant, Eliezer, some servants and ten of Abraham's camels loaded with all kinds of good things on this trip to find his son a bride. This servant set out for the town of Nahor where Abraham had relatives. After a very long trip, Eliezer arrived at Haran and had his camels kneel down near the well outside the town. It was toward evening, and he knew it was the time each night the women came to draw water. He had in mind to study the women who came for water to see if he could find Isaac a bride.

Eliezer prayed, "God, make me successful this day. May it be that when I say to a young woman, 'Please let down your jar that I may have a drink, she will say, 'Drink, and I will water your camels too.' That will my sign to let her be the one you have chosen for your servant Isaac."

Before he finished praying, Rebekah came from town with her jar on her shoulder. The young woman was very beautiful and a virgin. She filled her jar from the well and placed it back on her shoulder.

Abraham's servant, Eliezer, hurried to meet her. He said, "Please give me a little water from your jar. I have traveled a long way, and I am very thirsty."

"Drink, my lord," she said. She quickly lowered the jar from her shoulder and gave him a drink. After she had given him a drink, she said, "I'll draw water for your camels, too, until they have had enough to drink." So she quickly emptied her jar into

33

the trough, ran back to the well to draw more water. After a long time, she finally fetched enough water for all his camels, making many trips back and forth to the trough with her jar. Without saying a word, Abraham's servant watched Rebekah closely, thinking the Lord had made his journey successful. This was the woman he sought.

When the camels finished drinking, Eliezer took out a pouch attached to the sash around his waist a gold nose ring weighing a beka and two gold bracelets weighing ten shekels. He gave them to the woman as he asked, "Please tell me, is there room in your father's house for me to spend the night?"

Rebekah answered him. "We have plenty of straw and fodder for your camels as well as room for you to spend the night." The young woman ran ahead and told her mother's household. Now Rebekah had a brother named Laban. He hurried out to meet the man at the well. "Come, you who are blessed by the Lord," he said. "Why are you standing out here? I have prepared the house for you and a place for the camels."

So Eliezer went to Rebekah's house, and the camels were unloaded. Straw and fodder were brought for the camels, and water for him and his men to wash their feet. Then food was set before him, but he said, "I will not eat until I have told you what I have to say."

"Then tell us," Laban said.

Eliezer said, "I am Abraham's servant. The Lord has blessed my master abundantly, and he has become wealthy. He has sheep and cattle, silver and gold, male and female servants, and camels and donkeys. My master's wife Sarah has borne him a son in her old age named Isaac. Abraham has given this son everything he owns. And my master made me swear an oath. He said, "Go to my father's family and to my own clan, and get a wife for my son. I want you to know it is Rebekah I have chosen. I picked this woman because I prayed to the Lord that the one to marry Isaac would offer me water and give water to my camels. That was to be the sign for me. The Lord chose Rebekah to give me water."

Laban and Bethuel answered, "This is from the Lord. We

can say nothing to you one way or the other. Here is Rebekah. Take her and go, and let her become the wife of your master's son, as the Lord has directed."

Eliezer and the men who were with him ate and drank and spent the night. When they got up the next morning, he said, "Send me on my way to my master."

But Rebekah's brother and her mother replied, "Let the young woman remain with us ten days or so, then you may go."

But Eliezer said to them, "Do not detain me, now that the Lord has granted success to my journey. Send me on my way so I may go to my master."

Rebekah's brother and mother said, "Let's call the young woman and ask her about it." They called Rebekah and asked, "Will you go with this man right now?"

"I will go right now," the young woman said because she wanted to please God.

So the family decided to send Rebekah on her way, along with her nurse and Abraham' servant, Eliezer, and his men. The young woman and her attendant mounted the camels so the servant could take her back to Canaan.

Now Isaac had come from Beer Lahai Roi, for he was living in Negev. He went out to the field one evening to meditate. As he looked up, he saw camels approaching. At the same time, Rebekah looked up and saw Isaac out in the field, walking in their direction. She slid off her camel and ran to ask the servant, Eliezer, "Who is that man in the field coming to meet us?"

Hal darted a glance behind her when she heard the rustle at the back of the tent. The kitchen helpers were leaving as quietly as they could. Emma had explained to her they would leave when the Bishop got to the part of the story where he said Rebekah slid off her camel. This was the helpers cue that the ceremony was almost over.

Chapter 5

The bishop's voice brought Hal back to his story. "He is my master," the servant answered. So she took her veil and covered herself. When Isaac caught up to them, the servant told him all he had done. Isaac brought the young woman into the tent of his mother, Sarah, and he married Rebekah." Bishop Bontrager took a deep breath and looked around the tent. "Was it easy for Rebekah to leave her family, friends and home so suddenly and go to a strange far away land? Nah, and it hasn't been any easier for our sister, Hal, to give up her worldly life. She is blessed by God for being willing to please Him. We all will be blessed in the same way if we are willing, like Rebekah, to do what pleases God."

Hal tried to stay calm as the bishop looked down at John and her. She knew the wedding ceremony was about over. The next part would be when John and she participated in front of everyone. She clasped her trembling hands tightly together and hoped she didn't do or say anything wrong during her vows.

"We have two people here before us who have agreed to enter the state of matrimony, John Lapp and Hallie Lindstrom. If it is still your desire to be married Brother and Sister in the name of the Lord come forth," Bishop Bontrager commanded.

John and Hal stood up, joined hands and walked forward. They stopped in front of the bishop. Elton Bontrager looked at John and then Hal. "Do you both still feel as you did earlier this morning when we talked about you getting married?"

"Jah," John and Hal said in unison.

The bishop ask John to answer that they would remain together until death and be loyal and care for each other in adversity, affliction, sickness and weakness.

John nodded his head. "Jah."

Bishop Bontrager turned to Hal and asked the same of her. Hal answered, "Yes."

Elton Bontrager bowed his head in prayer.

Daniel had to stop watching or listening to the ceremony. For awhile, he ignored the forceful struggle in his trouser pocket that had been under way as Goliath protested his dark confinement. He didn't want to miss a moment of the wedding. Suddenly, the boy realized all movement in his pocket had stopped. Afraid that his frog may have suffocated, Daniel glanced down. His pocket was flat as a pancake. He patted his pocket just to make sure. Frantically, he peered around his feet and out into the aisle. What Daniel saw made him panicky sick. He was sure his face turned as green as that large bull frog hopping down the aisle. The frog might have gone undiscovered, with everyone's attention, on the wedding if the creature had headed the right direction to get outside. But no, Goliath was turned around in a room full of long skirts and shifting farmer shoes. He hopped toward the wedding party at the front of the tent. Right toward Mama Hal, Daed and the ministers.

Daniel was desperate to catch his frog before someone spotted Goliath. He slid to the edge of the bench. If he crawled down the aisle maybe no one would notice.

Noah, thinking his brother was antsy from sitting on the hard bench for almost three hours, put his arm out and stopped Daniel. He scolded in a whisper, "Stop rutsching around, Bruder."

Daniel's shoulders drooped. His insides burned with hopeless dread, knowing there was impending doom ahead. Nothing to do now. The frog was too far away. Daniel squeezed his eyes shut and bowed his head. He prayed as hard as he could. *I hate to interrupt at this very important time, but God please, please take a moment to help hide my frog. It will not take you long and then you can continue taking care of this wedding. Denke. I mean Amen.*

Daniel opened his eyes and searched for the frog, hoping against hope God heard his prayer and answered him. Maybe with a nudge from God, the animal slid into a hiding place somewhere. No one would notice one frog on the ground since the guests had their eyes glued to the Bishop and the wedding couple.

No such miracle had occurred. Apparently, God had his hands full with the wedding. At that moment, Daniel felt very much on his own and helpless. The frog still sat in the middle of the aisle for all to see while he contemplated which way he wanted to explore.

The Bishop's voice commanded to the congregation, "Now here are two people in one faith, John Lapp and Hallie Lindstrom. Those here to witness this wedding today speak now if you know of any scriptural reason why these two people can not be married. You should let yourself be heard now or forever remain silent."

As if on cue, the bull frog shifted to face a row of women. Daniel put his hand over his eyes but couldn't keep himself from spreading his fingers to peek. Goliath took a flying leap, intending to hurry himself on his journey to freedom. Assuming he had found a dark muddy bog near the pond, he landed in Stella Strutt's large black lap. A puzzled look crossed her face as the elderly woman felt pressure on her dress. She ducked her head to search her lap, spotted the frog and squealed as loud as an old sow fighting the others for the last bite of mash. Her hands covered her face to blot out the sight of the frog. Then Stella went into action as she stood up fast. The heavy set woman grabbed the material in her billowing black skirt with the intention of getting rid of the frog. She shook with such force the fabric flew up, slapped Roseanna Miller's face and covered her up. Roseanna pawed the skirt off her head and stared at Stella skeptically as she tried to make some reason out of the old woman's actions. Roseanna looked to the front and saw the shocked face of Bishop Bontrager with his mouth wide open. This was a poor time for Stella to have a fit right in the middle of a wedding. It was not good she had angered the bishop in the process.

With an odd in place jig, Stella bent forward and shuffled her swollen feet one way than the other to see where the frog landed. She spotted Goliath hunkered down near her left shoe and screeched, "Oh, no!"

Not realizing he was on his feet and in the aisle, Daniel spoke in a stricken voice, "Nah!" He feared for the safety of his pet. Stella was going to step on Goliath if she didn't quit hopping around. Daniel thought he'd spoken more or less a whispered prayer or just for Stella's ears. He guessed not when the guests swiveled their heads back and forth between Stella Strutt and him. From the curious looks he was getting, Daniel figured he must have spoken out loud.

The bishop, face suddenly redder than usual, looked very nonplused at the two of them. It was one thing for Stella to speak against this marriage. She was always negative about Hal Lindstrom and didn't mind voicing her opinion to the bishop on this woman or any other matter. He just hadn't expected her to wait until now to object when the wedding was almost over. It was quite another matter for John's son, Daniel, to speak up against the marriage. The bishop was as puzzled as everyone else in the tent. They all knew for a fact that Daniel loved Nurse Hal and very much wanted her to be a member of the Lapp family.

The bishop's back became stove poker stiff as he looked down his nose at the boy. He'd deal with Stella in a moment. First, he had to understand why Daniel objected. He raised his voice above the titters traveling from one end of the tent to the other and barked, "Tell me again, Daniel Lapp, that you object to this marriage and why?"

The sudden hush was far worse than all the whispers. Daniel felt his voice carry to all four corners as he wiped his sweat beaded forehead on his jacket sleeve. "Oh -- uh -- nah, Bishop. I do not at all object. I -- I want Mama Hal to marry my daed," he stammered. The boy glanced at Hal before he focused on nudging a clump of grass with his toe. One look at Mama Hal's stricken face was all he wanted. Her pained expression was almost more than he could bear. She, like the bishop, must be thinking he wanted to stop the wedding. Even worse was the anger on his father's face as the man stared at him. Daniel didn't think he'd ever seen his daed look that mad before. His stomach pitched and rolled. His mind tumbled through all the ways he was in trouble over that frog. His problems were bound to become worse when his daed and the bishop cornered him after the wedding to lecture and punish.

The bishop looked down his nose as he focused on Stella Strutt. She sank back on the bench. Leaning her head back to stare at the tent ceiling, she rubbed her forehead until it was a glistening red. In a critical voice, Elton Bontrager said, "And you Stella Strutt? What have you to say about this couple not getting married?"

The elderly woman straightened on the bench when she realized the bishop was questioning her. Her mouth opened as wide as it could get which was considerable. It was hard to tell if she was suffering from lack of oxygen like a beached whale out of water or trying to speak. With her thoughts on the frog, her eyes glued again to the aisle floor where Goliath was last seen. She certainly didn't want that creature to jump on her again, but if she could point at the frog, maybe she'd be forgiven by the bishop for this embarrassment. After all, none of this was her fault. Who ever heard of a frog roaming loose at a wedding.

Roseanna Miller patted Stella's arm, trying to bring the woman to her senses. She said in a low voice, "You must answer the bishop. He is waiting to hear from you."

Daniel worried that Stella, her face blanched white, was going to pass out any moment. If she fell in the aisle, she might land on Goliath. Stella sat broad enough. He didn't want her to fall off the bench and land on his frog. She would for sure flatten Goliath.

Slapping her plump, stubby fingers against her chest, Stella weaved forward and backward. To Daniel's relief, the elderly woman collapsed the other direction onto Roseanna. Flustered by the older woman's actions, Roseanna grabbed hold of her and struggled to keep the heavy woman on the bench as she implored, "Schwestern Stella, what ails you?"

Bishop Bontrager cleared his throat and tried to keep his voice calm as he said, "I take it there is really no objections by anyone here to this couple getting married. We can continue ----."

As if he had been asked his opinion, Goliath, frying pan nervous at all the human tension in the room, let out a loud, deep croak.

Daniel's heart sank into his shoes. Now the cat, er the frog, was out of the bag for sure. The commotion stirred up again. Snickering and whispering, people leaned over or stood up to look over heads to search in the aisle, trying to locate where the noise came from. The nervous frog hopped once then slowly crawled forward, continuing on his freedom mission. There was a loud rustle of material as women, in the frog's path, gathered their skirts tightly around their legs.

The bishop stretched to his fullest height to see over the wedding party chairs. In all his years of conducting weddings, he'd never lost control of one until now. No one had ever spoken up during a wedding ceremony. He couldn't understand what was going on. For some reason the congregation was in a dither. Stella Strutt was more ferhoodled than usual, and Daniel was marching in place from one foot to the other.

Bishop Bontrager looked solemn but his ruddy cheeks twitched when he realized what all the fuss was over. He was glad it was the frog that created this problem and not objection to John and Hal getting married. He had to get back in charge of this ceremony quickly. "Brothers and sisters, quiet down. Listen to me. In Genesis, God said, "Let the land produce living creatures according to their kinds. The livestock and the wild animals and creeping creatures that move along the ground. Now tell me, does this creeping creature that moves along the aisle belong to one of you?"

Daniel licked his dry, trembling lips before he said meekly,

41

"Jah, he is mine."

The bishop shook his head slowly and clucked his tongue. "Daniel Lapp, this was a grievous thing you did. Turning that frog loose to interrupt this solemn occasion. Will you catch that frog so we can continue?"

"Jah, Bishop, but I did not turn him loose. He got away from me." That produced whispering and low snickers behind hand covered mouths along with a stern look from Bishop Bontrager. With the bishop's permission, Daniel dashed after the frog. Goliath felt the breezy draft as the boy rushed at him. The frog, not wanting to be a prisoner in Daniel's pocket again, had other ideas. He sailed over the empty bridal chair and landed in the seat. Thank goodness for a sister that was not squeamish about wild pets. Emma, quick of hand, grabbed the frog. She twisted in the chair and held the struggling bull frog out to Daniel.

As he accepted the frog, he whispered, "Denke."

She answered him with a scorching look. Not gute. Now he had one more person mad at him. Worst one in the world to have angry with him might be Emma. She didn't ever forget. Holding onto the stiffening frog as tight as he could, Daniel tried to stuff Goliath back into his pocket.

"Please, not there, Daniel," Mama Hal pleaded. "You should set the poor frog free before he gets loose in here again."

"But, Mama Hal, you don't know how hard Goliath was to catch the first time," Daniel countered sincerely in a hushed voice.

"Take that frog outside and turn him loose now," said John very slowly in a much too quiet tone to suit Daniel.

"Jah, Daed." Daniel noticed the bishop had his eyes rolled toward Heaven. He hoped if the bishop was praying about the wedding, he included Goliath and him. He had the feeling he was going to need all the helpful prayers he could get on his behalf. The boy trudged with a heavy heart to the opening as snickers spread across the tent once more. As he walked outside to let his frog go, he thought about what this heap of trouble he was in amounted to. He'd have to sit through a lecture from the bishop for sure, and he'd be ask to do penance for his sin. His father was going to hand out an awful punishment that amounted to doubling his chores. For days, Mama Hal would be laying a pained look on him as she talked about him and his frog spoiling her beautiful wedding. His imagination wouldn't allow him to think how much Emma was going to make his suffer for the rest of his life.

Daniel put his frog down gently on the ground. He felt as if he had already started his punishment by suffering the loss of his pet frog. He said softly, "Good bye, Goliath. It has been nice knowing you."

The frog let out a triumphant croak and hopped in bounding leaps toward the barn, headed in the direction of the pond. Daniel hesitated at the tent opening. He didn't want to confront all those amused faces, but he knew he couldn't miss the end of the wedding. It just wasn't done. That would upset Mama Hal even more, and he didn't want to do that to her. He'd just have to be brave and suck up what ever happened next.

The guests watched Daniel soft foot it down the aisle. Some snickered softly. *Not a good sign,* Daniel surmised. If he was in the bishop's shoes disrupting a wedding was unthinkable. Losing control of the congregation was an added insult. Daniel wished with all his might he hadn't caused all this fervor. He glanced at the bishop's bowed head. The man was still praying. Daniel hoped it was a patient, thoughtful prayer and somewhere in it the bishop mentioned forgiveness for him.

Daniel sat down on the bench next to Noah. He glanced at his brother long enough to see he sat with his arms crossed, shaking his head in disbelief. Daniel looked at the ground, afraid to look at anyone. When he heard the Bishop say amen, the boy said in a trembling voice, "I am back, Bishop."

Elton raised his head and went on as if nothing had interrupted him. "Now we continue." He joined his hands over the top and bottom of John and Hal's hands again. "Then he quoted from the book of Tobit, "And he takes the hand of the daughter and puts it in the hand of Tobias." Elton blessed them with "The God of Abraham, the God of Isaac and the God of Jacob be with you together as a couple and give his rich

43

blessings upon you and be merciful to you. To this I wish you the blessings of God for a good beginning and a steadfast middle and may you hold out until a blessed end. This all in and through Jesus Christ. Amen. Go forth in the name of the Lord. You are now man and wife."

John and Hal returned to their seats, looking calmer now that the ceremony was almost over. The bishop asked Preacher Yoder and Deacon Yutzy to express their thoughts on the wedding ceremony. They each took a few minutes to wish the couple God's blessings. After the two men finished, the bishop asked the bride's father to say a few words.

Jim stood up. For once in his life, he found words hard to come by. "This is a very important occasion for all the Lindstrom family. Hal's mother and I are excited. We look forward to being a part of this couple and their children's lives. We appreciate that you would let us be here for our only daughter's wedding. We are glad that you spoke in English so my wife and me could understand the ceremony. It meant so much to us. Thanks to all who helped worked so hard to get prepared for the wedding the last few days. We appreciated their work. My wife and I wish our daughter and her new family a blessed and happy life." That said, he sat down.

Bishop Bontrager stood. He asked the congregation to kneel in prayer. Everyone stood and turned to face their bench before they knelt. The bishop read the prayer out of the Christenpflicht prayer book as it is done at the close of Amish church services. The prayer was a little long, but he'd expected the ceremony to be somewhat shorter than it turned out. Since the prayer was picked before hand, the bishop didn't want to exchange it now for another one at the last minute.

The congregation rose but remained facing backward for the benediction. Then they turned around for one more hymn, and the wedding was over. Time for people to leave. The young people exited before the wedding party so as quick as he could Daniel got into the middle of that group and made his way outside. He intended to hide out of Daed, Mama Hal, Emma and the bishop's sight for the rest of the day.

44

Chapter 6

The wedding ceremony was over at mid day, but there was still a lot more celebration to go. Several of the young people that left the tent before the bridal party had to help with the preparations for dinner by being the waitresses and waiters. With a good size crowd like this one, it took two waiters and eight waitresses for the tent. Three young married couples, the *ech leit* or corner people, were assigned just to wait on the bridal party seated in the corner.

The cooks didn't get to see much of the wedding service. Four married couples were assigned as cooks. Most of the morning, they stayed with the food they were preparing. Three married couples were in charge of cooking the potatoes and warming other dishes. These were the couples that remained in the tent until the bishop got to the part where Rebekah slid off her camel. When they heard that cue, they headed for the kitchen.

From long experience, the cooks knew if the potatoes were started to cook at that time they would be soft enough to mash by the end of the wedding service. The cooks wanted to be able to go in and out of the kitchen during the service. They sat at the back of the tent so they wouldn't disrupt the ceremony. As luck would have it, all of the kitchen help slipped back into the tent in time to be present when the actual vows were said. Of course on this particular day, they were witness to the unusual and uninvited guest, Goliath. All thoughts about food preparation went out of their heads. They hated to leave until the excitement was over so they stayed a little longer than normal. It was agreed among the helpers that they might never see another wedding quite like this one.

As soon as the tent was empty, each man set up a table made with three benches placed side by side and elevated on a special trestle. As the tables were completed, a woman came along with a white tablecloth to cover them. The tables were place end for end in the shape of a U with the corner, the *eck*, of the tent, reserved for the bridal party.

Next the workers carried in large chests filled with unbreakable dishes and eating utensils. These chests were only used for large crowds at weddings and funeral meals. Several men in the community had the responsibility for storing the chests at their house and renting them out for an occasion. The plates and silverware were stacked on the end of the food table in the middle of the tent. The line of people could fill their plates from both sides of the table.

To save time, some of the smaller items were passed from the kitchen to the tent bucket brigade style. By the time the long table was filled with bowls and roasters, the cooks had carried out large amounts of food in a particular order. The main dish, several large roasters containing stuffing mixed with chicken pieces came first then ten gallons of mashed potatoes, and ten quarts of gravy. The traditional wedding dish was creamed celery along with twenty quarts of cole slaw and fifty quarts of applesauce. Deserts were thirty cherry pies, four hundred of Roseanna Nisely's doughnuts, fruit salad, tapioca pudding and the standard fare of bread, butter, jelly and coffee. For decoration ever so far apart on the tables, celery stalks with the leaves attached like a flower and stem were arranged in quart canning jars, a symbol of good luck.

On the *eck* table was a large cake, decorated with white icing, baked by Emma as her special contribution for the newlyweds. Small bowls held nuts, candy, mints and fancy fruit as well as platters of lunch meat and dip for the crackers. Holding hands, the couples entered the tent in the same order they did for the wedding. The ech corner was where John and Hal headed with the other couples in the bridal party once they past the food table. John and Hal sat across the corner from

46

each other, with Hal on John's left just like the way they would sit in church or a buggy.

One long table was meant for parents, grandparents and younger family members. Hal's father sat at the head of that table. Hal's mother sat on the side of the table along with the girl relatives under sixteen years old. On the other side, were the male youngsters which consisted of John's sons, Noah and Daniel and Mark and Rose Yoder among others. All the young people over sixteen ate together while the other wedding guests sat at the remaining tables.

After everyone sat down, they paused for a silent grace before they ate. Hal was surprisingly hungry, but why not. She'd barely eaten for two days. The tent filled with the lilting hum of the Plain guests talking as they ate the good food. They should have an appetite, too. Men and their sons were up before daylight to milk and do the other chores while the women and their daughters cooked breakfast and cleaned the kitchen. Before they knew it, they needed to get dressed in their Sunday best, hitch of the horse to the carriage and make it to the wedding on time.

The waiters and waitresses scurried in and out of the tent, refilling bowls, pouring drinks and supplying other needs. After the meal was over, everyone paused for another silent prayer before they left the tent. Now it was time for the helpers to fill their plates and sit down. The corner waiters and waitresses, according to tradition, had the honor of sitting in the *eck* to eat as soon as the wedding party left the tent.

This was the social time. Guests stood around in the yard, visiting until the tables were cleaned.

As soon as the helpers ate, they were assigned for clean up detail. Plus the waiters and waitresses had to wash and dry the dishes. A couple of them pushed into the tent a double galvanized washtub filled with soapy water on one side and rinse water on the other. One woman brought in a large stack of dish towels. While the dishes were washed in the tent, the other set of helpers washed the dishes in the kitchen.

When the cleanup was over, women moved back into the

tent so they could sit down to visit, and the men went to the barn. The younger children ran away from the others to play softball. The teenagers separated, the girls to Emma's room upstairs to visit and the boys down by the barn to play darts.

After about an hour, Emma stood in the tent opening looking for Hal. When she spotted Hal, she made her way among the guests. "Hallie, we have the wedding gifts on the bed in the spare room. You can come upstairs and open them now." She spoke in a louder voice to the women, "Komm with us while Hallie opens her gifts."

As soon as they reached the spare bedroom, Emma led Hal to the bed. They waited for all the women to fill the room. Hal was surprised to see how many white papered gifts covered the bed. As she opened the gifts, she found that though the gifts were new and practical. In a few minutes, the bed was covered with Tupperware containers, crystal salad and fruit bowls and kitchen utensils.

Each gift had a slip of paper attached with a pin to the wrapping so she'd know who gave her the gift. She opened a large gift and ran her hand over the most beautiful quilt she'd ever seen - red rose buds appliquéd along the light cream fabric. Rose buds were attached to each other by green tendrils. A row of tendrils vined along the scallops around the outside edge and a heart shaped ring filled with rose buds was in the middle. The name on the slip of paper was EMMA.

"Emma, this is so beautiful. You out did yourself putting together this lovely quilt. So much hard work. How did you find the time? Where have you been quilting this that I wouldn't see it? Where did you hide the quilt that I didn't come across it?" Rushed out of Hal's mouth.

Emma giggled. "Slow down, Hallie. Jane helped me work on the quilt at her house. When you went to work, I went to visit Jane. She said I should leave the quilt at her house until the wedding so you wouldn't accidentally find it."

"Oh denke, Emma. What a treasure this gift is." Hal gave Emma a hug then turned to Jane. "Denke for helping Emma." Then Hal spoke to all the other women. "Denke for your thoughtfulness and for all the gifts. Each one will be a special reminder of you."

"Now look over in the corner at what your folks gave you to go along with the quilt," Emma said.

A large cedar quilt chest glowed with an amber glint caused by the sun shining through the window on it's downward journey. "This is a wonderful gift, Mom." Hal opened the chest. She sniffed and got a whiff of cedar that would permeate the stack of quilts she'd put in the chest. That is if she ever figured out how to make them. At least, she had Emma's wedding quilt to start with. Funny, Mom hadn't put a big bow on top the chest to make it stand out from all the other gifts. Emma must have clued Nora in to the fact only a small slip of paper was appropriate. The paper said Love Mom and Dad.

Hal continued to unwrapped a few remaining gifts. Each time, she exclaimed how much she liked the item. When she finished with the last one, she turned to the women around her. "The real gift for John and me is that you are all here to enjoy this day with us. Now I should go back to my husband and see what happens next. Please, join us downstairs."

For awhile, John and Hal moved among the clustered guests, handing out candy bars as they visited.

"See my sisters sitting over there." John nodded mid way of the tent as he touched Hal's elbow. "Let's say hello." The two women 's dark hair coloring and eyes were very much like John's. There was no doubt in Hal's mind that they were related to her husband. John smiled down at them. "It is so voonderball gute, Beth and Amy, that you could both come today."

The ladies stood up. Beth, slim and wiry, gave him a hug. "We would not have missed this wedding for anything in the world. Would we, Amy?" She gave Hal a hug and patted her back.

"Ach, nah!" said Amy, a plumper, shorter version of her sister. She stood on tiptoes to hug her brother than Hal. "Wilcom, to our family, Hal."

"Denke, I'm proud to be a part of the Lapp family," Hal

49

assured them. "Denke to both of you for all your hard work yesterday. We so appreciated it. I don't have to fear spiders for a while now, and I can actually see out of the windows when company comes."

The sisters giggled behind their hands.

Amy said, "You are wilcom."

Beth turned serious. "John, we were disappointed our bruder, Marvin, ain't here today."

"I just got a letter from him yesterday. He said he couldn't come this far right now. One of the twins is sick with a summer cold. He figured the other will come down with it soon. You know how that is with kids," John said with a chuckle.

"Ach, I guess we do," Amy agreed adamantly.

"Hal said we should write Marvin and tell him his family is wilcom when the boys are well enough to travel. They can come any time they want," John said, putting his arm around his wife's waist.

"Voonderball gute! Will you let us know so we can visit with Marvin and Ida when they are here," Beth said excitedly.

"Of course, we will," Hal said. "I'm hoping they can stay long enough to visit around the neighborhood. You should come for meals and spend as much time as you can with us while they are here."

"Denke, Schwestern Hal. We will look forward to that," Amy said. "It has been a long time since we last saw Marvin and his family. I can't remember how long. When do you think, Beth?"

"Right after the twins, John and Marvin, were born two years ago. Remember, we paid a driver to take us to see the new babies."

"That's right," Amy agreed.

Bishop Elton and Jane Bontrager approached the newlyweds. Elton shook John's hand and Jane hugged Hal. They both spoke to Beth and Amy.

"What a nice wedding ceremony, Elton. We really appreciate what you've done for us today," Hal said, giving the elderly man a hug.

"Gute," was Elton's one word reply.

John looked grave when he spoke. "Elton, I am so very sorry for what Daniel did. We have yet to talk to Stella Strutt and see if she is all right. The poor woman must be very upset."

"Jah, I saw her earlier. Stella was still beside herself," Jane said, and she giggled behind her hand.

"Boys will be boys. Stella has forgotten what it is like to have small ones around that are full of life," Elton said, grinning at John.

Amy said cryptically, "Knowing Stella she will forget this matter and be upset with something else shortly."

"Jah," Beth agreed. "That is Stella's way."

"Just the same, Daniel's bad behavior troubles me," John said seriously. "He is always tempted to act before he thinks."

"John." Amy gave him a weak smile. "Daniel is just a little boy, but he reminds me very much of you at his age."

"I agree, Schwestern," said Beth, with a solemn shake of her head. "I remember hearing much the same words come out of our parents mouth when John did something that they disapproved of. Daniel is a son very much like his father."

"That may be, but I remember punishments Daed handed out for my unwise actions. I can not let this latest problem with Daniel go unpunished. He will not learn how to act the right way if I do," John said firmly to his sisters.

"What you decided is up to you as his father." Elton paused then suggested, "Would it help if I as bishop had a talk with Daniel."

"It was your wedding sermon the boy interrupted. If you want to talk to him I would be grateful," John said. "I would like Daniel to be more responsible for his actions, and he does respect your wisdom. In fact, he probably expects you will want to talk to him." John grinned as he rubbed a sideburn. "I do not think you should disappoint him."

Mid afternoon was the time for the young people to sing for the wedding party and guests. The long table had been set with snacks: chips, fresh platters of celery, red and yellow apples, and three kinds of cookies heaped on plates. On one plate was stacked the remainder of the delicious doughnuts Roseanna Nisely worked so hard on. Hal picked up two of them so she'd get her fill. She knew that plate would be the first one emptied.

Just before the singing, the boys went one at a time into the upstairs bedroom where the girls were. Each boy stood in front of the girl he wanted to sit by at the singing and held his hand out for her to take. Holding hands, they walked downstairs and went into the tent. For the afternoon, boys that dated one girl on a steady basis didn't have to pick her for the singing. Later in the evening, the dating couples paired up and spend the rest of the time at the Lapp wedding together. This way a boy had a different partner in the afternoon to get acquainted with.

So the young folks sat in pairs at a couple tables, talking. They waited for the wedding party to sit down in the Eck corner and the guests to find seats. John and Hal were serenaded while they opened the few wedding gifts left for them on the table. These gifts were considered novelty items. Noah and Daniel had made miniature buggies from marshmallows with lifesaver wheels hitched to animal cracker horses with toothpicks. Several people had gift wrapped bowls of candies in plain white paper.

From time to time, John and Hal heard the words, "Knock, Knock." The tent wall waved back and forth by the split in the corner. Either John or Hal would stick a hand through the crack to give a child, they couldn't see, a piece of candy. This activity reminded Hal of Halloween.

Hal smiled at John and reached over to pat his hand. She whispered, "This has been the most wonderful day, John Lapp."

"That is the way I see it, too," he said, grinning at her.

The Forgeher (ushers) handed out the Ausbunds, thick German hymn books, which only had words, no musical notation.

Hal frowned at the singing table. "John, there's that strange young man by Emma."

John glanced that direction and said unconcerned, "Jah, Josh Beiler."

Hal had a different reaction, but she decided to keep it to herself. Emma was sandwiched between Josh and Levi Yoder. The girl looked uncomfortable with her arms tightly penned against her sides. Josh slanted his body enough that his shoulder seem to bore into Emma's. To make matters worse, Levi was paying more attention to the young girl he had chosen. A sight that Hal didn't like to see. All right, that's the way it should be between Levi and the girl next to him, but Hal wished Levi would have had the good sense to choose Emma at a social function like this.

Hal felt sorry for Emma. For one thing, the way Josh smiled at the girl was just plain wrong. He reminded Hal of an Amish Phil King. Emma should have been Levi's choice. Hal was sure of that. How had Josh gotten to Emma before Levi could pick her? For a young man that seemed so bashful around others, Josh sure was forward with Emma. This young Plain man didn't seem to have a bashful bone in his body when he smiled at Emma. Whatever he said to her in the pause between songs made her blush. He was a stranger in the community and didn't really know Emma or any of the other girls well enough to be that forward with them. At least, that was Hal's opinion.

What started out in the usual chant like manner for the first song changed to a tempo that was faster in the next songs as the afternoon wore on. The girls could help lead the singing if they wanted to at this gathering. Their sweet young voices blended together with the boys. Hal never grew tired of hearing hymns like *Amazing Grace* and *How Great Thou Art* even though the words were in the Plain dialect.

Later that afternoon, some of the guests left for home to do chores. They hurried home so they could get back in time for the evening meal. For other neighbors who lived farther away, the day had been long enough. They decided not to come back.

At five o'clock, the bride and groom left their table, ending the singing. The snacks were cleared away by the afternoon crew which consisted of aunts and uncles and young married couples that went to church with the couple. The groom's family, Amy and Beth, pitched in. After the workers cleaned up the tables in the tent, the evening servers warmed up the leftovers from dinner, heated wieners to go along with pork-n-beans and poured potato chips in bowls for a lighter supper. Ice cream was dessert. Before the servers waited on everyone else, they ate their meal at the kitchen table.

Emma had told Hal the duty of making a list of young unmarried couples that sat together for supper and the evening singing fell to the bride. She claimed it wouldn't be a hard job. When asked, many of the boys picked the girl they dated on a regular basis.

Hal suddenly decided she didn't mind the task at hand. She had a plan since she was determined to make sure Levi was paired with Emma for the evening. This task gave Hal the opportunity to stop another young man from picking Emma, especially Josh Beiler. When Hal went upstairs, she found the boys standing at the end of the upstairs hall, ready for the pairing. As Hal walked over to the group, she searched for Beiler. He wasn't with the boys. Maybe he'd went back to the Yoder farm to do chores. She hoped he stayed there.

Hal stopped in front of Levi Yoder first and insisted, "Levi, can I put Emma as your choice for the meal and evening singing?" That wasn't a choice for Levi, but Hal wasn't taking a chance that he'd choose someone else.

Hal smiled with relief as Levi agreed enthusiastically. "That would be gute."

She noted Emma's name next to Levi's on her paper. "Enjoy the evening," she said as she stepped in front of another boy. Suddenly, she felt someone too close behind her. Near enough the hair stood up on her neck. Hal twisted quickly and her shoulder bumped Josh Beiler's chest. Her eyes met his intense brown ones that was trying to burn a hole through her.

"Hallie Lapp, I am a stranger here. Perhaps, you would like to *pick* a girl for me, too." Josh's words carried all the meaning they needed to tell Hal he was unhappy with her interference.

As if to lend protection, Levi moved closer to Hal. She turned to him and asked innocently, "Levi, would you like to suggest a girl for Josh?"

"Nonni Stolfus," Levi said quietly.

Their eyes met again as Hal turned to Josh. She didn't have any intention of backing down so she spoke with deliberation. "That will be your girl for this evening."

He shrugged his acceptance, and she moved away from him. Though she felt the need to be cautious around this young man, she was determined not to let Josh know how much his demeanor bother her. She jotted down the names of girls the boys dating on a regular basis gave her. Bashfully, each one ducked his head as he uttered the name he wanted her to write next to his.

This social event was one of the very few times the parents of these couples saw them together. It was always a source of interest to see these almost grown children's date choice. Other people craned their necks to see what young man liked a certain young woman enough to choose her to sit with in public. The couplings made fuel for speculation for some time to come about future weddings.

Hal returned to the tent when her job was done. She sat down and wished for a fan to circulate the heavy air. After a day of August sunshine bearing down on the canvas, the air was weighted with heat at supper time. The wedding party again were in their places in the corner as far away from the entry way and any breeze as they could get in a packed room. Knowing she couldn't have a fan, Hal decided to wish for sundown. Darkness would be a welcome relief.

One of the eck waiters, Andy Zook, brought in three new cakes and placed them on the table. Hal gave her list of paired couples to him. The young man took his job serious as he positioned himself between the upstairs bedroom the girls were in and the gathering of boys at the end of the hall. In a loud, clear voice, he read the names of the couples paired on the list one couple at a time. Each boy walked to the bedroom door as the girl came out of the room. They went down the stairs, holding hands.

Another waiter for the Eck corner waited for the young couples to show up at the opening. He seated the couples at their table. The pairs going steady but didn't have plans marry had to be seated on the groom's side of the table. Couples that had just married or planned to be married this wedding season sat on the bride's side. At other tables were relatives and friends of the couple.

Just before they sat down to eat, Hal and John had prepared special bowls with treats of cake, fruit and candy for their special wedding helpers. Everyone had worked so hard to make this day special for the bride and groom. The gifts the ushers, cooks and the bishop received from them would not be much in return. The real repayment, John told Hal, would come when they returned the favor by helping at weddings when they were called upon.

The young couples had to share the dish of ice cream which made this a special treat. It was always a bashful moment when the couples tried to decide which one of them would get the last bite. Hal noted in the case of Josh and Nonni, there wasn't that uncomfortable moment about which one of them had the last bite. Looking bored, Josh pushed the bowl in front of the long faced, freckled girl. Elbow on the table, he sat with his head against his hand and watched Nonni enjoy the last of the ice cream. It would appear Levi had picked the right partner for Josh. She was one girl that was safe since this full of himself young man wasn't interested in her.

Levi looked over at the ech table. When he saw Hal's pleased expression, he lean forward and glanced down the table to see how Josh and Nonni were getting along. He caught Hal's attention, gave her big smile and slightly nodded he understood. She winked to show she approved.

Just as they finished eating, hymn books were passed out that were used at Sunday evening singings. Together they sang, "What A Friend We Have In Jesus". After several more selections, one by one the guests started leaving for home. By ten thirty, there were only a few people left.

The left overs were set on the kitchen table for a late night snack. Emma came to the tent to let everyone know that the fress (to eat gluttonously) table was prepared. Singing stopped.

After the last of the guests ate, the men went out to hook up their horses to their buggies. The women cleaned up the kitchen, washed the dishes and put away the leftovers.

Emma pulled Hal aside. "You and me have to go upstairs to the spare bedroom and do something with the wedding gifts before my dawdi and mammi get ready to go to bed."

"I guess we should," Hal said and giggled. "It wouldn't be very comfortable sleeping in a bed filled with wedding gifts."

Giving some thought to what would be the quickest way to clear the bed that late at night, Hal decided, "Emma, can we stack the gifts in the storage closet in the spare bedroom until some other day when we have more time to deal with them? I'd hate to ask the women to wash another dish or container tonight now that they're ready to leave just so we can put things away in the kitchen."

"That is a gute idea," Emma agreed.

When Emma following her. Everyone had gone home. They were alone at last. Hal sighed deeply and smiled at her parents and the boys, sitting together on the couch, " What a day!"

"A voonderball gute day, but tomorrow is clean up day so we will have plenty of company again," John warned.

"This is as late as an old man like me can stay up," Jim said, covering a yawn. "Too much excitement for one day."

"You are very tired. I know," John said.

"We all are," Nora said. "I can tell from as quiet as we all are."

"Would you like to stay for the evening prayer before you go to bed?" John asked.

"Of course, we will," Nora agreed.

"We all kneel in a circle," John explained. "I think this special night with all our family together we should say the Lord's Prayer. As soon as everyone was down, he began, Unser vater der du bist im himmel, geheiliget werde dein name zu komm, uns dein reich, dein viille geschehe auf, erden vie im himmel, gib uns heit, unser taglich brod, und verbig uns, unsere schuld, vie wir vergeben, unsern schuldern; und las uns nicht, eingefuhrt weden in verschung, sondern erlose uns von med osen, denn dein ist das recih, dein ist die, kraft dein ist die herrbichkeit in Ewigkeit. Umen.

"Amen," the others echoed.

"Now show me to my bed. I have to get some rest so I'll wake up early enough to milk cows," Jim said, grabbing hold of a nearby chair to help himself up from the floor.

Emma laughed. "Come with me Dawdi Jim. I'm headed to bed myself. Let me show you and Mammi to the spare room."

Noah got up to follow them. Daniel shadowed at Noah's heels, trying to get away.

John said sternly, "Daniel, I would like a word with you."

The boy froze. Noah gave his brother a look of pity and keep going up the stairs.

Hal touched John's arm as she rushed by him. "I'm going up and get ready for bed." She glanced at Daniel long enough to get a you're deserting a sinking ship look. Hal felt sorry for the boy, but she was smart enough to know there would be times John had to use his judgment when it came to disciplining his children. He wouldn't like her interfering. Most of the time, John was the very image of a mild and loving parent, but he managed sternness very well when the occasion warranted. She knew that from experience when she'd displeased the man.

When they were alone, Daniel moved in front of his father.

"I feel as if you have been avoiding me all day, Son," John began. "It is not hard to know why I think."

"Des verschtehn ich," Daniel groaned.

"You understand now? It is too bad you did not understand before hand instead of after you disrupted a very solemn occasion for Mama Hal and me and everyone at the wedding," John scolded.

"I did not know I would be interrupting by keeping Goliath in my pocket. I did not have any place else to put him," Daniel said with tears in his eyes.

"So be it, but do you realize you are guilty of a wrong doing?"

"Jah, I do, and I'm very sorry," Daniel said mournfully.

"That is a start, but only that. You must tell Hal you are sorry and the bishop, too. Elton said to tell you he wishes to speak with you about this matter as soon as possible."

Tears trickled down Daniel's cheeks. He had expected as much. It was one thing to have friend, Elton, upset but another when he had angered Bishop Elton Bontrager. "W – what is going to happen to me?"

"I am not sure how the bishop will handle this matter. That is for him to say. As for me, I am going to assign you extra chores until I am sure you have repented for this grievous error. Is that understood?"

Daniel swallowed hard. "Jah."

"Now go to bed. We have a busy day tomorrow." John watched as the boy raced up the stairs to get away from him. The thought ran through his mind if he thought Daniel was a handful now, what would he be like when he was a teenager during runspringa?

Chapter 7

The next morning, Emma's roosters took their duties seriously as the farm's feathered alarm clocks. They took turns crowing as soon as the bang of the back door woke them up. The men and boys were already on the way to the barn. The women were in the kitchen getting breakfast started, but the roosters didn't know that. They needed to earn their keep by waking people and animals on the farm. All they succeeded in doing was to stir up the hens. The flock sang their cawing song while they waited for Emma to come feed them.

The household had to hustle to beat the arrival of company. In a short while, the extensive clean up was under way. Hal's mother pitched in to help Margaret Yoder do the laundry. Emma heated the pails of water for the wash and had loaves of bread rising on top the warming oven to bake for lunch. Margaret carried the steaming pails out into the mud room and filled the gasoline motored wringer washing machine. Nora carried cold water in from the pump out back to fill the rinse tub. There was several loads to wash with all the tablecloths, dish cloths and towels they dirtied up at the wedding. When Margaret let Nora know she had a basket full ready to dry, Nora helped her hang the laundry on the clothes line.

As Nora penned a tablecloth, she glanced anxiously at the overcast sky. "I sure hope that's just temporary."

Margaret nodded agreement as she took a clothes pen out of her mouth and secured a tablecloth corner. "And if it isn't, the least the rain could do is hold off until we can take the laundry down. As warm as it is, won't take long for everything to dry. We'll keep a close eye on the laundry and take it in as soon as we can."

Linda Yoder cooked lunch. Emma and Hal packed the dishes they had left stacked on the counter overnight back into the chests. Someone had to return the chests to the people who were in charge of them. With all the help, much of the work was expected to be done by noon. Men came to take down the tent and put all the benches back in the two bench wagons. Emma put the boxes of hymn books in the back of each wagon. One wagon went to the farm where the next Sunday meeting would be held and the other back to another district.

Mid morning, Nora wiped her sweaty brow and let out a tired sigh, before she wiped the table where she'd peeled potatoes.

"Mom, why don't you sit down a minute. We're about done here. You should rest. You've been on your feet all morning. Doesn't help that today is so warm." Hal wiped sweat beads off her own forehead and then rolled her sleeves up to her elbows. Didn't help that the kitchen stayed heated with water boiling and food cooking, but she knew better than to complain. No fans or air conditioner allowed.

"Better yet, why don't you come with me to see my chickens, Mammi Nora," invited Emma. "The fresh air will help us both cool off, and I've been wanting to show you my flock."

"Getting some fresh air sounds like a great idea. Thank you," Nora answered.

"Can I come see the chickens?" Hal asked.

"Ach, nah, you know what the chickens look like already. Keep working," Emma commanded playfully as she winked at Nora. "I want a moment alone with my new mammi."

After the back door banged shut, Margaret smiled. "Hal, I think the children are taking to your folks well."

"I hoped they would," Hal said, dunking a mixing bowl in the rinse water. "My parents have hinted for a long time they wanted grandchildren before they died. Now they instantly have three."

"The Lapp children needed a set of grandparents. Your

61

parents are perfect. Too bad they live so far away," Margaret said.

"If you only knew my parents, you might rethink that idea," whispered Hal seriously.

Margaret giggled. After she saw how serious Hal looked, she laughed.

What Hal said about her parents wasn't all that funny. Why did Barb and Margaret laugh when she tried to confide in them? She was fairly serious about her parents living across the state being a good thing since they didn't know very much about the Amish yet. She started to say so, but stopped. Margaret had her hand clamped over her mouth, staring behind Hal.

Hal looked over her shoulder. She took her hands out of the dish water and turned around in slow motion. Water ran off her hands and dripped onto the floor. She glanced down at the gleaming drops in front of her feet and quickly dried her hands on her apron.

Sporting a goofy grin, Jim Lindstrom had slipped up behind her. Hal stared at the hat he wore, a size too large Amish felt hat that rested on his ears. Mystified, she asked, "Dad, what are you doing with that hat on?"

Jim said gleefully, "I'm thinking of trading John for it even up. To take the place of my new western hat you said I couldn't wear around here."

"What did you trade John?" Hal asked suspiciously. Out of the corner of her eyes, she caught a movement in the kitchen doorway and heard a familiar snicker. Behind her Margaret began giggling uncontrollably. John leaned against the door facing with his arms across his chest. Her father's white western hat was perched on top his head. Obviously, the hat was too small, but John didn't seem to care.

Hal was dumbfounded. She looked from her father to John. Her husband grinned from ear to ear as he watched Hal's face. Margaret tried to contain her giggling to no avail, and Hal felt ganged up on. Who knew John and her dad would tease her like this?

She focused on her dad when he explained, "John, is going to take me for a ride to show me around the farm. I needed a hat on my head in this hot August sun so John was kind enough to loan me his. John needed a hat too so I loaned him my western hat to see how he'd like it since I can't wear it."

"Oh by all means, the two of you go have *fun* and a good, long ride to the back forty," Hal said evenly.

Through the open window, she heard her father on the front porch say, "Don't think this hat trade is gonna work. You have a big head, son-in-law."

John burst out laughing. "You are right. I am thinking your head is voonderball, awful small."

Hal peeked around the curtain and watched as the men took the hats off and traded back.

"Margaret, now you see what I tried to tell you. It's a good thing my parents live so far away. If for no other reason than John and Dad would drive me crazy if the two of them lived close together," Hal said through thin lips.

Margaret snickered and wiped her tearing eyes with her apron tail. "What I see is two men comfortable being together and trying to shake the new bride out of her sudden seriousness. It appears over night you have turned into a Plain person with no sense of humor. Go with this voonderball experience, Hal. Enjoy your parents while they're here and put up with the two fun loving men in your life. Be glad they like each other and get along so well."

Hal smiled weakly. "You're right as always. Now are you going to finish drying these dishes or do I have to do that job, too?"

Just then Nora and Emma came back inside. Emma hustled over to the stove to stir a pot. She didn't look happy.

"Well, what do you think of Emma's laying flock, Mom?" Hal asked, feeling uneasy as she watched Emma.

Nora sounded impressed when she said, "The hens are really nice ones. She's raised some great looking pullets that should start laying this fall."

"I think so," Hal said. "Emma, are you all right?"

63

"Es ist nix," the girl said.

"All right. If it's nothing, why do you look upset?" Hal asked bluntly. Had her worse fears came to pass? Had her mother unintentionally brought up something from Aunt Tootie's book of Amish Customs that offended the girl? Or had Emma told Nora the awful story about the pet rooster Hal accidentally killed? Maybe, Emma grew upset all over again at the thought of her beloved rooster's demise. "This have anything to do with a certain rooster?" Hal asked, eying Emma.

"Ach, nah. One of the young ducks has returned from the pond. He is still trying to sit under the mother hen's wings. Can you believe that?" Emma asked, disgusted. "It just does not seem there will be any end to this foolish prank my brothers played."

"No way! One of those little ducks came back again?" Hal asked, trying to look serious. "What are you going to do?"

"As soon as I see Noah or Daniel, one of them is going to catch that duck and take him to the far end of the pond again," Emma said with determination.

Meanwhile free to play for the moment, Daniel and Mark Yoder walked down the driveway, looking for something to do. Daniel stopped to study the hog pen board fence. "Bet you can not walk the top of the pig pen fence clear around it without falling off. I do it all the time."

"I can do it if you do it," Mark boasted. He was the same age as Daniel and an inch taller. His edge in height over Daniel gave him the idea that he could be better than Daniel at anything. "I'll bet you are just saying you can stay on that fence."

"Komm and watch me," Daniel invited. "But you have to walk the fence, too."

The two barefoot boys climbed up on the top board. They edged along, Mark behind Daniel, wavering back and forth with their hands stretched out tightrope fashion.

The sows gathered to watch, squealing and shoving each other away from the trough. They thought it must be time for another feeding. A really loud squeal caused Daniel to look down as one sow bulldozed another out of her way. He wobbled to one side and became over balanced. Next thing he knew he was in mid air. The hogs watch him sail in their direction. They emitted frightened screams much louder than Daniel's cries. With a squishy splash, the boy landed in the squalid wallow the hogs enjoyed when they wanted to cool off. The hogs riled up the dusty pen, escaping to a safe place in the far corner. Once they bunched together, the hogs turned around. In unison, they protested this intrusion in their hog wallow.

The sight of his friend in the mud caused Mark to laughed. He slapped his knee as he asked, "Wie waar des?"

"How it is in this bog is not gute. It is voonderball awful smelly down here." Daniel scrunched up his nose.

"You picked a soft place to land," Mark said, choking on his laughter. Too late, he weaved too far sideways and lost his balance. Before he knew it, Mark was on his backside beside Daniel with the hog wallow's greasy black mire scumming up around him.

"Tell me now how you like it," snapped Daniel. He slapped the black mire as he tried to get his footing and slipped back down, speckling Mark's face and hair with flying mud.

The hogs grew curious. Maybe this commotion had something to do with food. The dozen sows edged over to the edge of the mire. They opened and shut their mouths, making snapping sounds between barks that let drooling slobbers drip in front of them as they sniffed the soured mud for eatables.

Daniel yelled, "Get away!" He said to Mark, "We have to get out of the mud before they a hold of us and eat us for lunch."

As Mark kept an eye on the agitated hogs, he struggled to get up, but he slipped back down deeper in the suctioning mire. His voice trembled as he said, "I can not get to my feet. We are not going to get out of here by ourselves."

"We need Noah and Levi. Help!" Daniel yelled.

Mark joined in. "Help!" One good thing was their loud voices kept the hogs at bay for the moment. The sows back up a few feet while they checked out this latest commotion. "Help us," the boys yelled together.

Levi came out of the barn with Noah. "What is getting the hogs worked up?"

"Hard telling," Noah answered. "Maybe one of the cats walked across the pig pen. The sows do not like that."

"Wait! I just heard someone call help," Levi said, breaking into a run for the pen with Noah right behind him.

They stepped up on the bottom board of the fence and looked down.

"What a mess the boys have got themselves in. We better get them out of there before the hogs get them," Noah said urgently.

Levi jumped inside the pen and squalled at the hogs. They raced back to the far corner and bunched up. Noah already had Daniel up and stepping out of the mire. Levi grabbed Mark's hands and tugged on him until he slid out on dry land. The boys, looking sheepish, climbed over the fence and started for the house.

Noah and Levi caught up to them.

"Want to tell us how you ended up in the sows mud hole?" Noah asked. He grinned at the muck on the boys and the murky trail dribbling off them onto the grass.

Daniel and Mark kept walking, ignoring him.

"They sure do not smell voonderball pretty gute," Levi offered, holding his nose.

"I expect Emma is going to say the same thing and not nearly as nice as you just did," predicted Noah.

The boys stopped at the bottom porch step.

Noah called, "Emma, I think you better come out here."

Levi put his hand over his mouth, trying to stop giggling. Noah had to turn his back to the house.

Emma opened the screen door. Right away she spotted Daniel and Mark. Her face creased up in horror. "What have you two done?"

"We fell in the pig pen is all," Daniel said, trying to sound innocent.

"The two of you are going to take a bath right now." Emma

saw the other two boys start to edge away. "Noah and Levi, stay put. I need you to help me."

"We do not want to give them a bath," complained Noah.

"Jah, they got into that mess. They can clean themselves up," insisted Levi.

"I agree," Emma said. "Daniel, go to the back door and tell Hallie you want some hot water for the bath tub. Tell her to set the tub in the back yard. *You* are not coming in the house until you are clean and smell gute."

"But I will not have anything to wear," Mark complained.

"You should have thought of that before you got yourself in this shape," Emma snapped then relented when she saw tears in his eyes. "Do not worry. I will get some of Daniel's clothes for you. Now scoot around the house. It is going to take awhile to get you clean, and we are busy. I did not need this to happen today," Emma groused. "Now Levi and Noah, I want you to catch one of those small ducks again. He has made his way back from the pond to the chicken house. This time see if you can convince him the pond is his home," she suggested strongly as she studied their shoes. On a roll, she pointed a finger at their feet. "You should clean off those shoes before you come in the house for lunch or take them off. Your hands can stand a good scrubbing to get the hogs stink off them, too. Use plenty of soap." Emma wheeled and marched back into the house to over see the bathing preparations for Daniel and Mark.

Chapter 8

That afternoon not long after lunch the cleanup crew left. The Lapp family was taking a breather. John and Jim sat on the porch steps. Each leaned against a post, relaxing for the first time in several days. The Yoder brothers along with Noah and Daniel sat in the grass, backs against the shade tree. In the living room, Hal and Nora leaned back on the couch with their eyes closed. Emma rocked slowly in the rocker.

Finally, Emma broke the silence. "We need to do something special this afternoon."

"Like what, dear," Nora said, opening her eyes. "I'm about specialed out at this moment."

"How about going on a picnic?" Emma suggested. "We can see if the men and the boys would like to fish in the pond?"

"That sounds like a great idea," Hal said. "Go ask your father. I'm sure he will say yes. Mom and I will get busy gathering the food."

"Where do you picnic around here?" Nora asked Hal as she followed her daughter to the kitchen.

"We have our own special spot on this farm, don't we, Emma?"

Emma smiled as she answered, "Jah, we can walk to it." She went outside. "Daed, we want to do something special while Dawdi and Mammi are here. How about we have a picnic and go fishing this afternoon?"

"What you think, Jim? You like to fish?" John asked.

"Why, fishing is my middle name. Let's go," Jim said enthusiastically.

Emma spoke loudly through the screen door. "They are

68

agreed." She turned back to the men. "We will be along in a while with a picnic lunch to eat in the grove. I will bring a can for the worms. Make sure to get a pole for me while you are at it. "

"I will." John walked over to the boys, "Did you hear that? We're going fishing. Boys, bring a shovel to dig some worms. I'll get the poles."

In a short time, the women carried the dish towel bundles out to the red wagon. Emma pulled the wagon as they walked down the lane. Hal pointed across the pasture. "Mom, see that grove of trees. That's our picnic grounds. The children keep a big area in the middle cleared so it's like a park. And the cows graze on the grass so it's always short. Makes for a pleasant spot to picnic and camp out."

"Sounds like it as long as you watch where you step," Nora said, grinning as she stepped around a fresh cow pile.

Emma giggled, tugging on the wagon with one hand and holding a can of worms in the other. "We do not think to tell the boys that often enough. Going bour feesich anywhere outside of the yard can be a problem when we have die coos loose." She stopped walking. "Hallie, are you limping?"

"A little. I don't have these new shoes broke in yet. I think I've blistered both heels," Hal groaned.

"It is about time you did what all the rest of us do. Take your shoes off and go barefoot in the summer," Emma told her. "Before you put those shoes back, put some band-aids on your heels until you get the shoes broke in."

"Sounds like a plan to me," Hal said as she slipped out of her shoes and leaned them against a fence post in the lane fence. "Now I'll be able to find them when we come back tonight. You want to take your shoes off, Mom?"

"No, I'll pass. My feet are too tender to walk barefoot," declared Nora.

"Take the wagon, Hallie." Emma handed over the tongue and took off ahead of the women. "I am going to find where Daed laid my fishing pole."

As Emma trotted away, Hal chuckled. "Emma loves to fish."

69

"Have fun and catch more than the men. I'd like fried fish for lunch tomorrow," Nora called after her. Quietly, she said, "You have wedded a lovely family, Hal."

"I did, didn't I? I feel so lucky to have them." Hal grew quiet for a moment, listening to the wagon wheels squeak through the grass while worries raced through her mind. "Mom?"

"Yes, Dear."

"Does it seem like to you I've changed a whole lot lately?"

"No, you are still our Hallie. You can't change from the person you are just because you dress differently." Once the words were out of her mouth, Nora hesitated and looked at her daughter. "Oh dear, I didn't mean that about your dressing differently in a bad way."

"It's all right. I understood what you meant."

Nora questioned, "What brought this on anyway?"

Hal looked serious as she studied her mom. "Something Margaret Yoder said when Dad and John were clowning around with their hats. She said they were trying to bring me out of the serious Amish person I had become back to the fun loving person they had always known. That surprised me. I didn't realize I'd changed."

"You haven't. Not really. I think you're just trying very hard to be the person you think the Amish community will want you to be. You are trying too hard to get accepted by everyone. Take my advice. Just be yourself. The person they have grown to know and love. The rules about what you can and can't do as an Amish person will come naturally after awhile. You won't be so worried about making a mistake." Nora grinned at her daughter. "Which should be some easier for you to do than it is your father and me since you don't have Aunt Tootie giving you lessons."

Hal blushed as she realized her mother had read her mind about Aunt Tootie's book of Amish customs. "Oh, Mom. You're always so wise. You know me pretty well," Hal said, tugging on the wagon handle to start it rolling again.

"I should. I've had lots of years to get used to you. You're new to the Amish community but that will change, too. Soon nothing you do will surprise the Amish once they get to know you. If it does, they will take it as a fluke of nature ingrained into Nurse Hal's character," Nora said with a tongue in cheek look on her face.

Hal stared at her mother. "Thanks a lot, Mom. I think."

"You're welcome. Now we best get ready for this picnic before it's time for the hungry fishermen to gang up on us," Nora said, picking up her pace.

They passed through the outer line of trees, filled with birds lazily calling to each other and by the blackberry thicket, Hal stopped and looked around. "This is the place. We need to pick up some sticks for a fire from under the trees. Roasting hot dogs and marshmallows will be a nice change after all the cooking we've done lately. I'm glad I bought an extra bag of potato chips last time I got groceries. This will be a perfect picnic."

"You're right, but it's all of us together, talking and enjoying each other's company, that makes the picnic special." Nora headed off toward the trees one way while Hal went the other direction. With an arm load of sticks, Nora started back to the clearing. Her toe connected with something that didn't budge in the tall grass. She snapped, "Ouch!" When she staggered, she dropped her sticks which clattered across the ground. Nora put her hand up against a tree trunk and managed to stay upright. All the noise brought Hal running to check on her.

"Mom, are you all right?"

"I am now except for a smarting toe. I thought I was going to be on my face for a second. I'm sure glad I had my shoes on. What did I stub my toe on?" Nora pulled apart the grass and saw the small wooden cross with the word Diane on it. Another cross was next to that one with Patches written on it. "What have the Lapps got here? A private family cemetery?"

"Well, it is and it isn't. There is a cemetery for the district that most of the Amish are buried in. That is where Diane Lapp is buried. Although I've seen a few private family burial places scattered about. Let me help you gather up your sticks. Once we get the wood piled, I'll tell you the stories about the crosses while we have the grove to ourselves," Hal said.

The afternoon passed quickly while Hal caught her mother up on the death of Patches, the family dog and how saddened they had been. She told her mother she felt the only way to make the children feel some closure about Patches death was to bury him with a private funeral.

More complicated was the story about what was under the wooden cross with Diane Lapp's name on it. Hal made her mother promise not to mention she knew the story to any of the Lapps before she began. While the women talked, whoops of joy when a fish landed on the bank and loud teasing about who had the biggest catch so far drifted to them from the pond bank.

Later that afternoon, John and his boys trudged toward the barn to milk. Emma, Levi, Mark and Jim continued to fish. Hal listened for the milking machine's rumble to stop. When the barn was silent, she walked to the edge of the clearing. John and the boys were headed to the picnic grove. Hal lit the little pile of dead leaves she pushed under the sticks. In minutes, the camp fire burned brightly and fast consumed the supply of dried wood Nora and Hal gathered. Hal and her mother went back among the trees to pick up more sticks. Hal threw her arm full on the fire. Nora dumped her sticks nearby for later and went to the edge of the clearing to yell it was time to eat. When John and Jim arrived, they fished their pocket knives out and cut some green sticks to use for roasting the hot dogs and marshmallows.

Nora said to no one in particular, "Were the fish biting today?"

"Jah," Emma said smugly. "Very gute."

"Mostly on Emma's pole," grunted Noah.

"One of us had to have good luck, Grandson or we'd not have anything to eat tomorrow," Jim teased, elbowing Noah in the ribs.

"I agree with Noah. Emma is too lucky at fishing," Levi teased, winking at Jim.

Emma blushed because of the off handed praises and ducked her head.

Soon everyone lit into the browned hot dogs in slices of Emma's homemade bread and bowls of chips while they sat around the blazing campfire.

The wind picked up as they put marshmallows on their sticks. The campfire flames wavered back and forth as the marshmallows swelled and browned, mesmerizing them all.

Sitting between Noah and Daniel, Jim suggested as he nibbled on his roasted treat, "Next time it rains, you two ought to get out after dark to pick up night crawlers. Those worms are easier to bait a hook with then the little red worms you dig."

Daniel licked the excess goo off his stick and grumped, "We never know when we're going fishing after a rain."

"Don't matter," Jim replied. "The worms will keep for awhile until you ready to fish."

Noah shook his head. "Not for us. We've tried, and the nightcrawlers always died."

"Did you put them in a cool place?" Jim asked.

"Nah, I don't think we have one," Noah said.

"Yes, you do. The root cellar is a perfect place to keep them," Jim said. "You have to put them in shredded newspapers and dirt. Make sure to sprinkle them with water often and feed them."

"Feed them?" Daniel snickered.

Emma grew interested. "What do nightcrawlers eat, Dawdi?"

"They eat all the stuff you have on hand. It's chicken feed, oatmeal, brown sugar and powdered milk. Mix a cup of each thing together and keep in a covered container. An old oatmeal box works well. Sprinkle some of the feed on top the worm bedding once a month. Why you might even be able to go into the nightcrawler selling business if you take care of all the worms you can pick up," Jim encouraged.

Nora perked up. The grumbling of distant thunder was just a little louder than the talking and laughter. "Listen, does that sound like a storm coming? Or am I hearing things?"

The others stopped talking and strained to listen.

John said, "You are not hearing things. Look through the trees at how gloomy it is in the pasture. We better go for the house, or we will be soaked. Levi and Mark, you head for home before the storm hits."

"Mom and Emma, you gather up our things. I'll go back with the boys," Hal said. "And gather up Mark's clothes."

She rushed across the pasture with the boys. By the time Levi had their horse hooked to the buggy, Mark was waiting, his arms filled with freshly washed clothes.

As the boys climbed into the buggy, Hal said, "Next time you come to visit, you can bring back Daniel's clothes."

Hal and the Lapp brothers waved at the Yoder brothers as they went out the driveway. Hal sat down on the top porch step where she could watch the growing storm cloud while she waited for the others to make it back from the picnic grove. Daniel plopped down beside her.

As he headed around the side of the house, Noah said, "Think I'll shut the chickens up for Emma right quick."

Quietly, Daniel reached over and slipped his hand in Hal's. He looked troubled. "Daniel, is something bothering you?"

The boy's dark eyes moistened. "I am worried that you are very upset with me for ruining your wedding." His voice trembled.

Hal put her arm around him and hugged him close. "You should know, Daniel Lapp, that I'd never be really upset at you no matter what you did. You must understand that I love you that much and a whole bunch more." She kissed his cheek.

"Des verschtehn ich, but Daed says I need to tell you how sorry I am for what I did," he said in a small voice. "To say so is part of my penance."

"Are you really sorry?"

"Jah, so really sorry," Daniel vowed, nodding his head.

"Well then, it is good that you've done what your father asked." Hal cupped his chin in her hand. "Listen to me. You really didn't ruin my wedding."

Daniel perked up, but he looked confused. "I didn't?"

"Between you, me and the fence post, that is probably the

only wedding around here in years that almost everyone had a good time at during such a long ceremony. Folks will remember for years the day they were at the Lapp wedding when Daniel turned the frog loose. Probably the only wedding they didn't doze off at."

Daniel gave her a relieved smile as he explained, "I didn't really turn Goliath loose. He just escaped on his own."

"I believe you, but that doesn't mean you're off the hook with everyone else. It just means I am not upset. I don't want to hear any more about your ruining my wedding. The wedding was a beautiful ceremony I'll treasure forever, because it joined me to you and the others in this family. That's how I choose to remember my wedding day," Hal said, patting Daniel on the back. "I'll make sure to tell your father that you have apologized to me as he asked you to. Now I've got to go back down the lane before it rains. I just remembered I left my new shoes against a fence post."

"I'll get them for you," Daniel said, sprinting away.

The others came to meet Daniel as they walked to the house in the dusky dark, watching forked lightning streak the gloomy sky. Thunder boomed every few minutes, increasingly louder as the storm grew closer. Just moments after they made it inside, a flash of lightning lit up the living room. John lit the oil lamp by his rocker. Strong thunder rumbled long and loud, rattling the window panes. A downpour of large drops pounded the porch boards as the rain moistened the dust. Everyone was content to settle down and too tired to talk. They listened, only half awake, as rain drops pattered against the windows.

In a few days, daily farm life set in with a passion for the Lapp family. John took to spending long hours in the field. The corn was ready to chop for silage to fill the silo. This was the winter feed for the milk cows. From the kitchen, Hal and Nora heard the corn binder coming closer to the fence in the back yard.

"Let's go see what's happening out there. I've never seen a corn binder at work," Hal told her mother.

"Me either," Nora said.

They walked behind the hen house, and Emma came from feeding the chickens to join them. Hal shaded her eyes from the bright sun beating down on them so she could see better. The horse drawn corn binder chopped its way across the field, making snapping sounds as the binder swallowed up the stalks. The gasoline powered engine chugged noisily. John sat on the metal seat and guided the work horses along side the two corn rows he wanted to chop.

The corn binder, with sickles in the front that clattered back and forth, sliced the rows of semi green stalks low to the ground. The stalks laid over onto the gathering chains that sent the plants up the chute to be bundled. A knotter mechanism tied the bundle, making a snapping bang as it cut the binder twine. The bundle went on its way over the edge of the chute.

John had hired Levi and Josh to help him with the field work. Jim insisted on going along to help, stating that this reminded him of harvest when he was a kid. Levi managed the team that kept the flat bed wagon close along side the corn binder. Josh and Jim stood on the edge of the wagon at the back of the binder. It was their job to catch and pull the bundles onto the flatbed wagon and pile them along the wagon bed.

Jim looked across the fence and gave a big wave to the women. Nora clucked her tongue. "Will you look at that old fool? You'd think he was still on the Titonka FFA float in the fourth of July parade in Algona."

"Mom, he's having fun," Hal defended.

"I see that. I just hope he's being careful," insisted Nora.

"I didn't know Dad got to ride in the parade," Hal said, watching the binder make the bend and move away from them.

"It was no big deal. The FFA students had him hold onto a small pig for them. He held it by one leg and waved with the other hand the whole parade. I couldn't hardly stand the smell of him the rest of the day. Don't see how anyone else could keep from noticing."

When the binder got part way back down the field, the wagon was full. Levi yelled to John to stop. The men rode the loaded wagon to the silo behind the barn. John hooked the conveyor belt beneath the silo to the PTO on the steel wheeled tractor. He stepped upon the tractor and started it. The conveyor belt moved smoothly to the chopper, and the big fan rumbled.

Daniel and Noah unhitched the team, led them out of the way and tied them to the fence. The loud noises and everyone moving fast made the horses nervous. Even from a distance, they stamped and shuffled their feet as if protesting the mechanical progress that threatened to replace them.

Hal came from the house, eager to get in on the work. She helped Josh and Emma slide the bundles over the edge of the wagon. Noah and Jim placed them on the conveyor belt. John's job was to cut the binder twine and pull it away from the bundle so the stalks could be scattered along the belt. If the stalks had been allowed to bunch up that would plug the chopper and stop it. The stalks rustled and groaned to the other end of the belt and rattled loudly as the shredder chewed them up. The blower roared as the corn pieces disappeared into the silo.

In the gusty, hot wind, small pieces of shaft from the dry corn leaves flew in swirls around the workers, plastering to their sweaty skin with an itchy sting. The air smelled of crushed foliage and moist corn bits, a damp, sweet smell.

Emma tugged on a bundle that caught under the end of another bundle. She was leaning backward with the effort as she tugged. If the bundle came free too suddenly she might have lost her balance and fell off the wagon. Seeing Emma had a problem, Josh, in two steps, was by her side, with his hands over hers, pulling the bundle free with her. She smiled at him and mouthed the word, "Denke." He gave her a dazzling grin as he kept his hands on hers for a long moment before he took the bundle from her. Emma turned back and reached for another bundle. With all the deafening noise around them, words were almost impossible to hear without shouting.

Josh kept smiling to no one in particular as he swaggered over to the edge of the wagon to give the bundle to Levi. Hal saw the exchange between Josh and Emma. That boy meant to leave a lasting impression on the girl, and it was one Hal didn't like. What worried her was, she wasn't Emma. It was more important what she thought about that young man. Did the young woman see through this stranger who Hal thought was as cocky as one of Emma's roosters?

The flat bed wagon was about empty. Hal sat down on the end of the wagon and hopped to the ground. She should get the men a glass of tea before they went back to the field. It wouldn't hurt to see how Mom was doing in the kitchen, either. She wasn't exactly used to the wood cookstove or where to find anything she might need.

This was just the beginning of fall harvest. As soon as their silo was filled, John would take the corn binder to another neighbor. He told Hal he'd help other farmers fill their silo. Later in the season, he'd help pick corn by hand. The farmers would stack the corn stalks in shocks in the field to dry for winter feed for stock cows. After the ears dried, they would husk the corn with a hook attached to a leather strap buckled around their hand to pulled the ears off. They threw the corn into a horse pulled wagon that had a back board attached so the corn would bounce off and fall into the wagon. As soon as the wagon was full, the men scooped the corn into a crib to store. Just hearing about all that work meant Hal wouldn't be seeing much of her husband until the harvest was over. The only way the farmers ever finished before the snows came was by helping each other.

Chapter 9

Several days later it was mid afternoon, and Hal had just finished cleaning the kitchen. Not much else she could think to do for the moment. Though the kitchen smelled delicious because of Emma's two loaves of bread baking in the oven, the room was miserably hot. Hal wanted away from the heat for a bit to cool down so she went to the living room. She flopped down into John's rocker and leaned back against the soft, folded quilt behind her. Letting out a gusty sigh, she decided she was content with the world around her. Trying to get comfortable and cooler, she gathered her long skirt up to her knees before she placed Emma's recipe book on her lap. For a moment, she longed for her shorts instead of the cumbersome, hot skirt.

Thoughts of cool shorts made her sigh in regret. Quickly, that emotion turned to guilt, because she had such thoughts. She excused she was bound to miss English comforts she'd taken for granted for so many years. Guess she could miss them all she wanted if she didn't say so out loud in front of Plain people. She couldn't get excommunicated if she kept the thought to herself. Anyway, she guessed she was safe as long as she didn't run into a Plain person that was a mind reader.

Hal laid her head back on the rocker, closed her eyes and listened to the silence. For the first time in days, she was alone in her home. Strange to think of the Lapp house as her home. Somehow it always felt more like Emma's domain. Not that Hal thought that was a bad thing. She didn't know sometimes how she'd manage without Emma to guide her. Housekeeping and cooking wasn't talents she was born with. She thought her lot in life was to be a nurse. She'd never have time to be domestic. Boy, was she wrong. Now she was going to have to learn how to cook and clean. Skills she'd ignored all these years for that was exactly what being a homemaker was to Amish women. A talented skill perfected from when they were little girls.

Hal's parents had left early that morning, headed on a six hour drive home. She missed them already. To her surprise, more than she thought she would. She heard the sounds of a buggy. John must be home from helping Samuel Nisely in his corn field. He thought they would be finished with the Nisely corn harvest before chore time.

The kids had gone fishing for the afternoon. The house was quiet, but that was a good thing. A very good thing to be able to sit down for a moment and enjoy the peace by herself. Hal picked up the spiraled notebook filled with handwritten recipes passed down from Lapp relatives to help Emma cook. She turned the pages. What she was looking for was one of Emma's recipes she might do without flubbing it up. If she had supper ready before the children came home, wouldn't Emma be surprised? Besides, Hal felt she should be doing more to help Emma.

The back door slammed. Hal jumped. The kids must be back early. As usual, Daniel made it to the door first. Quickly, she threw her skirt down over her legs before she got caught doing something considered wrong. She didn't want to set a bad example for the kids.

Instead, it was John who lunged into the living room. He shouted breathlessly, "Hal, come quick. The kitchen is on fire." A cloud of smoke floated around John.

"Oh my, Emma's bread!" Hal shot out of the rocker, letting the recipe book flop onto the board floor. She raced past John into the smoke and grabbed a couple pot holders off the stack on the counter. White smoke wavered upward as the wisps leaked from the top of the oven. Hal jerked open the door. A contained mass of smoke billowed out of the oven and puffed into her face. She breathed it in and choked. Coughing, she lifted out one loaf pan of black bread. She dropped it on the table then grabbed the other one.

"Oh, this is so very awful," Hal cried. Tears streamed down her face as she looked at John through the smoke. She grabbed a dish towel and flapped it in the air one direction than the other, trying to disperse the smoke toward the open window and back door.

"You forgot to watch for the bread to get done?" John asked.

"I thought I'd just sit down a minute. I didn't think it was that long ago I put the bread in to bake." Hal's voice trembled. She blinked her burning smoke filled eyes and wiped tears off her cheeks with her sleeve. "I'm too used to depending on the stove timer in the apartment and the one on the microwave. They beeped when the food was ready. There isn't a timer on this old wood cookstove to help me out."

"Ach nah, I have never seen a timer on the stove," John said, trying to commiserate with his upset wife.

"John, before Emma leaves home, could we have a gas stove installed? It would be so much easier for me to learn how to cook on," pleaded Hal, snapping the dish towel in his direction.

John dodged as he agreed, "All right, if the boys and me are not to starve to death that would be a gute idea."

Quickly, she added, "And a gas refrigerator too." Before John had time to think about her rushed request, she demanded, "Now quick, go get a shovel!"

So urgently commanding was Hal's order John obeyed. He got as far as the outside door in the mud room and came back. "What do you want a shovel for?"

"I've got to bury this bread before Emma gets home," Hal insisted frantically.

John shoved his hands in his pockets and quizzed. "Why?"

"I remember my mother telling me a story about a cake she baked when she was first married. The cake fell. Aunt Tootie and Uncle Frank were coming for lunch. She didn't want them to see how awful the cake was so she threw it under the front porch and baked another one."

John couldn't figure out where this story was headed. He

81

scratched his sideburn as he said slowly, "Hal, our front porch is boxed in at the bottom. You can not throw a cake or the bread loaves under there."

"I know that. That's why I intend to bury the bread, because throwing the cake away idea didn't work for Mom. You see our dog, Trouble, dragged Mom's half eaten cake out and dropped it at Aunt Tootie and Uncle Frank's feet. Of course, they had questions, and Mom had to confess. Uncle Frank has teased the daylights out of her ever since, and that happened years ago. Uncle Frank never lets up if he gets something on you. Remember that from now on."

"I will, but I do not think your Uncle Frank will be coming to visit any time soon. If he did, you are not to worry Hal. We do not have a dog anymore. Remember?" John asked in a quiet tone, sounding much too patronizing to suit her.

Hal paced around the kitchen, waving the dish towel and darting glances out the window to make sure the kids weren't in sight. "Please stay with me on this, John. Burying the bread has nothing to do with a dog."

"But I thought you just said ----," John began, looking more confused if that were possible.

Hal interrupted, "I don't want Emma to come home and see the bread she worked so hard on looking like two lumps of coal. She's not going to be happy with me."

"I think it would be better to cut the black crust off and save the insides. Maybe Emma can figure out a use for the middles," John said sensibly.

Hal scrunched up her face as she stared at the black loaves and wavered. "You think so? I don't see how she could use brunt bread."

"Jah, I think it would not hurt to ask her."

Hal hesitated then declared, "Oh no, I'm not waiting for her to come home and see the mess I've made of her bread. Take these two pot holders."

As she thrust the pot holders in his hands, John raised one eyebrow. "Why?"

"If you won't help me bury the bread, you're going to help

me dump these loaf pans behind the hen house out of sight. We can only hope the chickens get rid of the evidence before Emma gets home. Be careful the pan is very hot yet," Hal said, putting one pan in John's hands and taking the other. "Hurry up now. The chickens won't have long to get rid of this mess before Emma gets back." She backed out the screen door and held it open until John came out.

John asked, "Where is Emma?"

"I sent her fishing with the boys. They were going to the creek. Emma hasn't had free time to have fun for so long. I thought if I could get the hang of cooking, which at this point I admit looks hopeless, maybe Emma could relax just a little and have fun."

"Maybe you should keep Emma home as much as possible while you still can," John said, eying the burnt bread as he dumped it. He watched the loaf bounce and roll across the ground.

"Emma's going to have the same thought I'm afraid if she thinks she can't trust me to do such a simple thing as bake bread," groaned Hal.

John nodded. "That maybe, but Emma will be 16 in three weeks."

"She will? You should have said something before this. That information couldn't come at a worse time. I don't know how to bake a cake from scratch yet for her birthday," Hal moaned.

John put his arm around her shoulders and tried to sympathize. "It's not so important that she has a cake. "

Hal pulled away from him. "It is too important Emma has a cake for her birthday. Do you know I don't know any of your birthdays? The boys will need one, too. I'll bet none of you have had a birthday cake in years. I want to change that. You have to tell me all your birthdays." Hal rambled more to herself than to John. "I don't know where my head has been. I should have thought to ask about birthdays sooner. Well, I have no other choice. Until I learn to bake a cake from scratch, I'll buy a cake for Emma this one time." She glanced at John to see if he was listening. He had crossed his arms over his chest and was giving her a look that said she'd gone haywire. "Oh okay, I know that's cheating. All right, I'll get a cake mix and make the cake myself. Mixes are practically fool proof these days." Then she muttered on the verge of tears, "I hope anyway. Of course, I'll have to babysit that dragon belching stove until the cake is done so I don't burn it, too."

"Come with me." John insisted firmly as he got her by the elbow and led her back into the house. "Hal, please sit and talk to me. You have to calm down. Emma will be back soon to help you. I can not figure what is the matter with you, but you have not been acting like yourself for days. I think you are sick, or you would not be so upset. What is wrong? You go from being sick at your stomach in the morning to flighty as a nervous filly at the least little thing the rest of the day."

"That's the way it is for women expecting," Hal admitted, wiping her sweaty face on a potholder.

"What are you expecting?"

Hal's gaze shifted to his face as she whispered, "A baby, John Lapp."

John took her face in his hands. "We are having a baby! How long have you known?"

Hal paused to think. "I knew a few weeks after that night when that bundling idea of yours failed. For your information if Emma ever mentions bundling in a bed with a boy, I'm going to tell her to say no. Although I can't be sure. Maybe this happened on our all night camping."

John looked worried. "Why did you not say something before? Do you not want a baby?"

"Sure I want a baby, but I've been really worried about telling you. I wasn't exactly sure how you would take the news. It seems I get in trouble so easy with everyone around here. If I am in trouble about this I'm warning you right now, you should stick up for me. Me being pregnant is half your fault."

"Why would anyone not like you having our baby?" John said, confused.

"Do Amish people spend much time counting back if a baby comes seven months after a wedding?"

John grinned. "Nah, it happens, and no one seems to notice once the couple is married. I am glad and voonderball relieved. This news helps me know why you have been so ferhoodled."

Hal studied the potholder in front of her, thinking about the burnt bread again. "You know you may be right about keeping Emma around here as long as we can. I have a lot to learn and taking care of a baby is one. I don't expect Emma to know much about that at her age, but perhaps, Margaret or Jane can give me advice while Emma makes a cook out of me. That is if Emma isn't too upset at me after today. She just might be ready to give up on me as a temperamental failure." Hal winced.

"Now stop worrying about Emma. She is more than willing to help you learn to cook, and you did right to let her go fishing. It is gute the boys have her to watch them even though they can swim. Daniel might try to catch another frog and fall in a hole. The creek is deep in spots," John said.

"Emma has help with that job. Levi is with them. He certainly has a level head on his shoulders for a young man, and he can swim. I asked him just to make sure," declared Hal.

"Now it is you that is missing the point. Sixteen is when Plain girls start dating. Emma will be able to come and go as she pleases soon. You will have to figure out how to manage in the kitchen when she is not here. Levi is around so much. He may be thinking about becoming more than just a fishing friend sooner than we would like," John warned.

"Oh, you're sounding like a father. Levi is just a friend Emma grew up with. She thinks of him as another brother. He's ----," she searched for the right word. "Harmless."

John shook his head. "I was a teenager once. Trust me. No boy Levi's age is harmless."

"Relax. Emma has never shown any interest in boys. She's been too busy taking care of you and her brothers to even think about dating, and now she has me added to her workload," Hal declared, wondering if she was trying to convince herself as much as John. As if somehow she could put off the inevitable. She sure hoped Emma leaving home was not going to happen any time soon.

85

"That can change mighty fast, Hal. There are several eligible young men in this community that will be paying attention to Emma one of these days. She is a good catch," John warned, trying to prepare her.

Hal said, "Spoken like a proud father. Don't worry. I'll learn to do the kitchen duties and especially don't worry this time. If I know Emma the only thing on her mind is besting the boys at fishing."

Daniel's excited voice interrupted from outside. "Mama Hal, come here." The four children were on the porch steps. "Look at our fish," Daniel said as he and Noah held up stringers lined with bullheads and bluegills.

"You had a good afternoon," Hal praised them.

Grinning, Levi teased, "Ach nah, Emma did. We were about ready to send her home or not give her any more worms. That right, Noah and Daniel?"

"Jah." Noah nodded.

Daniel agreed as he glared at Emma, "That is right."

Emma quietly grinned from ear to ear.

Hal elbowed John in the ribs and whispered, "What did I tell you? We worry too much."

"*We?*"

"That's what I said. Now my problems about what to fix for supper have been solved, too. Care to stay and help us eat fried fish and biscuits, Levi? It's the least Emma can do. Feed all of you hard working fishermen her catch."

Chapter 10

In the night, the sound of a sudden rainstorm woke Hal. A steady flow of rain rattled down the drain pipe and emptied into the cistern. Puddles still stood in the driveway when Hal looked out after daybreak. As soon as John finished the milking, he came to the house. Grabbing a cup, he poured coffee from the pot on the back of the stove. Hal wondered what was going on. It wasn't like John to stop for a coffee break since the harvest started. He took a sip as he studied her. Finally, he said, "Hal, how about we go visiting today?"

"Why?"

Emma explained, "Hallie, that is what newlyweds do right after they get married. They spend time with relatives, visiting. Sometimes, they stay all night. It is easier to get from one place to another."

"John, don't you still have field work to help with?" Hal asked.

"That is right, but it is too muddy to be in the field today. This day I want to take you to meet Esther and Eve Weber. Don't fix lunch for us, Emma. I thought we might eat with the Weber sisters," John said.

"Are they relatives?"

"Nah, just gute friends."

"Sounds like fun," Hal said.

Emma agreed, "It will be. The Weber sisters are friendly, and the best cooks around here."

Once the carriage was rolling down the road, Hal relaxed and watched the countryside slide by. It was a good feeling to get away from home for awhile and do something different with John. The trees glowed with a slight touch of autumn splendor. Oak trees were a mixture of yellow and green leaves, weeping willows turned pale green and maples burned red. She leaned against John, lulled by the buggy's steady rocking rhythm. Ben's hooves echoed on the pavement, but when John turned off on a gravel road the clip clopping became muffled in the damp earth.

Puffy, mountainous clouds moved slowly above and in front of them in the fiercely blue sky. Crows and sparrows sailed back and forth above the buggy. Red tailed hawks sat on fence posts, paying no attention to the movement of travelers. Their only concern was finding their next meal in the grassy road ditches. The southern breeze wasn't too warm, and gave some relief from the sun. It would be a different story in the afternoon when the sun rays baked down on them as they traveled home. The breeze would cease and leave them in summer mugginess.

Suddenly, Hal thought of Emma at home alone and felt guilty. Here she was enjoying herself. Once again, she'd put all the household responsibility on Emma. "I feel like we should be home. I should be doing something to help Emma," she worried.

"Both of us will make up for taking the day off tomorrow," John told her. "It is part of Plain folks way to go visit as many of our family, friends and neighbors right after we get married as we can. They need to get better acquainted with you. This helps everyone get used to us as a couple. Now that your parents have gone home we should move on with our customs."

"Sounds like a good idea. Visiting with Plain people will help them get to know me. They might feel easier about using the clinic. Though they tried to help, Jane and Margaret's quilting frolic idea didn't turn out so well thanks to Stella Strutt," Hal suggested.

"Jah. Hal?"

"Hmm."

John cleared his throat and said flatly, "Now that we are

alone, it might be a good time to have a talk."

Hal groaned as she moved away from him so she could see his face. "I'm not sure I like the sound of that. What have I done now?"

"You should know that your mother thought I should have this talk with you." The corners of John's mouth twitched in good humor.

"Oh no! What did she say? You have to forgive her. Aunt Tootie put some weird ideas in her head about Amish Customs from a library book of all things."

"It has not been so long ago that you wanted to get a library book to learn about Plain People as I recall," John said to rub it in. He glanced at her long enough to see the disgusted look on her face and spoke quickly before Hal could do more than open her mouth. "Anyway, Nora said you had forgotten how early you had to get up on a farm since you have become a nurse. My mother-in-law said I would have to explain to you how early you need to get up so you didn't shirk your duties."

"That's not true," Hal said with a steaming red face. "I know how early the day starts. She's right about me being raised on a farm, and my memory is not that short."

"According to Nora, it makes a difference that you were raised on an English farm and not a Plain one," John straightened out.

"It doesn't make one whit of difference which farm I was raised on. Besides I've stayed in your house enough before we were married to know what your daily routine was like," Hal defended.

"That is also true, but I was the man about to marry Nora's daughter. After you warned me about your parents not liking the idea of us sleeping together before we married, you don't think I was going to tell your mother that fact, do you?" John said, winking at her.

Hal gave him a squinting look. "Good idea. You are a smart man, John Lapp. Say while we're on the subject of my parents, tell me what was that hat swap all about with my father?"

"That is the second thing, I was to talk to you about. Your

daed said you did not like him wearing his new western hat at my house," John said seriously.

"That's not exactly true. What I said was he couldn't wear that white cowboy hat to the wedding. It wouldn't be appropriate. I didn't mean he couldn't ever wear it," Hal said exasperated.

"Perhaps Jim misunderstood," John conceded. "You should explain this to him. Just so you know, your parents are always wilcom in our home. Whether they come with Aunt Tootie's book or a cowboy hat does not bother me. I enjoyed the time we spent with your folks, and I want them to come back soon. I appreciate the fact that from the two of them you were born. It is because of them, I have you in my life."

"Ah denke, John. What a nice thing to say. I thought you liked my mom and dad, but it's nice of you to say so." Hal wrapped her arms around John's arm and kissed his cheek. "Now tell me again about these sisters we're going to visit," Hal said. It was time to get off the subject of her parents before he thought of something else they had warned him to remind her about.

"The Weber sisters are our version of a cafe. Many English people eat at their house to experience what Plain cooking is like. Most of the food they serve is raised in their large garden. Neither one has ever married so this is their way of making a living. They can the excess vegetables like all Plain women so they have enough food for themselves during the winter," John told her.

"I see. So does this mean you're taking me out to eat. Sort of like a date?"

"Perhaps an English person would call it that. We just call it visiting. If we are to buy a meal at the Weber sisters we have to do it through the week so this does not happen often. They do not serve on Sunday, and that is when we do most of our visiting. Operating a business on the Lord's day is forbidden, but we can visit them on in between Sunday afternoons like we will other families," John explained. "Hang on. We're coming to a branch."

When Ben put his front hooves in the shallow, sparkling water, he hesitated slightly before he stepped lightly through the rippling currant. A white farm house was in sight just ahead of them. The two sisters, Esther and Eve, waved at them from the porch. They didn't seem very surprised to see company drive in. Hal always wondered what sixth sense kept Plain people aware of what was going on in the neighborhood. Maybe they all had a touch of ESP, and in that case, she best be careful what she thought about in front of them.

These two sisters were as different as day and night. Brown haired and short, Esther had a bell shaped figure, and ash blond Eve had a long bony face attached by a slender neck to a willowy body.

The women invited the couple in and seated them at the table. Chattering away, Eve served them hot tea then continue to bustle around the large kitchen with her sister, preparing a lunch for their visitors. On one counter were large, saran wrap covered tinfoil pans of cinnamon rolls and light bread rolls, ready for customers that ordered them ahead.

After Eve checked the bubbling pans on the stove, she asked Hal, "Would you like to see our garden?"

"Oh yes. Emma is teaching me about putting in a successful garden, but I fear I have a lot to learn. Are you coming, John?"

"Nah, I will talk to Esther while you look," he said.

Esther, not one to waste words, waved her hand as a dismissal and poured herself a cup of tea so she could sit with John.

The two women walked past a chicken house with a fenced pen full of busy hens. They walked on a path used so often grass no longer tried to grow. Eve opened the garden gate and led the way around the grassy edge that bordered the garden. "I hope everything is going well at your house now that the wedding is over. That is such a busy time, and maybe not easy for you when you are just learning our ways."

"Everything went just fine with all the help we had. My parents have gone home now. The house is much quieter so it's a good thing that we're all busy. I love this new family of mine.

Now I just hope the community accepts me so I can help everyone that could use the clinic that John built on the house," Hal said, hoping to find an ally in Eve.

"Jah, Esther and I will be sure to bring that up to others for you," Eve agreed.

"Denke so much." Hal stared at the garden, amazed at all the rows running long ways and filled with every imaginable vegetable. "You have such a large garden and so clean. You must spend a lot of time out here."

"Jah, our hoe handles have grooves in them that fit our hands quite gute," said Eve with a smile.

Hal laughed then a thought came to her. "Emma says you have a bakery. You must spend an equal amount of time in the kitchen."

"Jah, we have customers for our bread and rolls that don't stay to eat a meal," Eve said.

"How about cakes? Like birthday cakes. Do you make them?" Hal asked excitedly.

"Jah."

"Could you make me a cake for Emma's birthday? I'm nervous about something going wrong if I try to bake one. I'm not much count in the kitchen as a cook yet. Emma is teaching me, but not in time for me to make a cake from scratch for her," Hal confided.

"Jah, we can do that. It will cost ----."

Hal interrupted, "I don't care what the cake costs. I'm so glad to find a way to get a homemade cake for Emma's birthday. Can I come and pick it up the day before? That would be September 15th." As Eve nodded, Hal said, "That way I can spend the time on her birthday getting ready for a family party."

"That will be fine, and do not worry about learning to cook. It will come in time. A cake is actually an easy thing to make," Eve assured her. "Now we best go back so I can help Esther with lunch."

After Hal and John ate all they could hold of baked chicken, mash potatoes and gravy, chicken and noodles, fresh bread and apple pie, Hal pitched in to help the women clean the kitchen.

When that was done, John said, "We should go. It will be milk time soon." He turned to Esther. "How much do I owe you for our gute meal?"

"Nothing," the sisters said together.

"This meal is our wedding present to you," Esther added.

"What a nice gift," Hal said as she gave each of them a hug.

"Denke, Sister Eve and Sister Esther," John said as he shook hands with them. "We will come again some Sunday afternoon to visit."

As they drove away, the sisters waved good bye and shouted, "Come back soon."

That evening, Elton and Jane Bontrager came to visit after supper. Once the talk about the wedding day died down, Elton assumed his Bishop demeanor. He looked over at the boys playing scrabble on the table by the window. "Speaking of the wedding reminds me while we are here, I would like to have a private talk with Daniel."

Daniel stiffened and grimaced at Noah. He laid a scrabble piece down on the table and scrunched up in his chair as if making himself smaller would make him invisible.

"Is it all right that we have this talk in the kitchen, John?" The bishop asked.

"Jah, Bishop. That would be fine," John agreed solemnly.

Elton winked at John and Hal before he turned and held out his hand to the boy. "Come along, Daniel. You and me should talk for a while by ourselves."

"Jah, Bishop," the little boy said meekly as he shuffled along holding Elton's hand.

Elton smiled at the boy and invited, "Sit down with me at the table." After Daniel slid into the chair next to the bishop, the elderly man folded his hands on the table and said, "So tell me, are you happy to have Nurse Hal as your mother?"

Daniel smiled as he said, "Jah, Elton." His smile faded. "I meant Bishop. I am sorry."

"That is all right. I know how hard it is to keep friend Elton separate from Bishop Bontrager sometimes," Elton said kindly.

Daniel's expression was earnest as he studied the bishop. "You do?"

"I do. It happens to me all the time. So you know the difference, right now I am Bishop Bontrager."

"Jah," Daniel said meekly.

"I have a reason for this talk. I felt it was gute before too much time has past for us to discuss the matter of your frog joining the wedding ceremony uninvited," Elton stated.

"Uh ---- oh, I was afraid of that. Bishop, I did not know Goliath was going to hop out of my pocket. I am sorry he did that," Daniel declared.

"It may be that you are sorry, but would it have been a wiser idea to put the frog -- er Goliath somewhere he would be confined better than your pocket until after the wedding was over?"

"Jah, it would have been a much better notion, but Bishop, I could not think of a place to keep him on such short notice. I just caught Goliath the day before," Daniel reasoned.

The bishop looked down his nose at the boy. "I see. Where did he spend his first night with you?"

"I turned him loose in the bedroom with Noah and me for the night." The bishop gave him a sideways look. "I shut the door so he would stay put until I found him the next morning. He was sitting under the bed pretty as you please. Goliath did not hurt a thing and was so gute. He did not croak once to wake up Emma or Mama Hal and Daed." Daniel paused before he stated solemnly, "Until during the wedding that is."

Bishop Bontrager tapped the table with his fingers. "Jah, he had a gute loud croak he used right in the middle of your parents wedding ceremony. I do not blame Goliath for wanting out in the fresh air. The poor frog could not breathe in your pocket. Daniel, do you agree bringing the frog to the wedding was a mistake?"

"Jah, I do agree," Daniel said seriously.

The bishop said, "There are several things you need to do to make your things right for this disruption of your parents wedding. I wonder if you have done any of them. Have you apologized to Stella Strutt about this matter? That poor woman was quite scared and very upset about the frog causing an embarrassment for her in front of all the congregation."

"Nah, I have not seen Stella since then, but when I do I will be glad to tell her how sorry I am that my frog jumped on her," Daniel offered contritely.

"Is that all you should do?"

Daniel looked puzzled then added almost as a question, "I will say I am sorry I scared her."

"Is that all?" Elton asked.

Daniel was baffled. "What else should I do?"

"You should tell your mother and daed that you are sorry for your actions. Goliath caused a disturbing interruption to their wedding ceremony," Elton instructed.

"That I have done," Daniel said quickly. "Daed has given me extra chores to do as my penitence, and Mama Hal forgave me."

The bishop looked at him sternly. "Gute. Now you have to do something for me. Promise you will not bring Goliath to Sunday meetings."

"I will not do that ever. I can not do that even if I wanted to," Daniel vowed sadly. "I turned Goliath loose outside the tent like I was told to do, and I have not been able to find him since."

The bishop's mouth twitched ever so slightly at the corners. He cleared his throat and said seriously, "I am sorry for your loss. Let me be clear about what I just said to you. You are not to bring any creeping creature, frog, snake or any other, in your pocket to a Gemessunndaag meeting, a wedding or a funeral. Is that clear, Daniel Lapp?"

"Ach, jah! I understand," Daniel said sincerely.

The bishop wagged his finger at Daniel. "Keep in mind this thought when you start to do something that might not be the right thing to do and you know it as such. What you do today, you will have to sleep with tonight. I am sure because of what you did you have not been sleeping too gute since the wedding," the bishop surmised.

"Ach nah, Bishop, I have felt terrible bad about what I did. I will not forget what you have said to help me," Daniel declared.

The bishop patted the boy's hand. "Gute. Something else I am curious about and would like to ask you. Does Nurse Hal talk on her phone a lot?"

Daniel puzzled over an answer. "Nah, I have not seen her use it at all."

"Where does she keep the phone?"

Daniel struggled to remember. "In her nursing bag in the clinic I think. I never see it."

"Gute. Now while I am here I want to see you say you are sorry to your folks as part of your penance." Daniel started to object. "I know you did this once but not in my presence. Go do this for me so I know that you are truly sorry," the bishop instructed.

Chapter 11

One evening in late August. Hal delighted in listening to summer sounds coming through the living room screen door. Living here was so totally different from the apartment in Wickenburg. In town, she'd been closed in. The only sounds were the rumble of the air conditioner, and cars.

Living in a house with a screen door and dim lighting, a person could imagine being outside in the evening in the fading daylight without having to put up with mosquitoes or gnats. The green peepers yeeped, and crickets rubbed their scratchy legs. Moths fluttered against the screen and lightening bugs glimmered just beyond the porch.

An owl hooted, causing Hal to jump. The bird was perched close. The children had already gone to bed so Hal and John had the living room all to themselves. Hal carried a chair over by the rocker so she could sit close to John.

"That owl is really close," Hal said, patting John's knee.

"He's high in the shade tree, looking down on us. Probably smells the chickens. Gute thing they have a building to live in. That owl would be eating one right now," John told her as he concentrated on the newspaper.

"John?"

"Jah?" he said absentmindedly.

"School will be starting soon. We need to do something fun for a change as a family while the children aren't in school," Hal said. "The summer has gotten away from us."

John put the newspaper, *Die Botschaft,* down on his lap. "What did you have in mind?"

"How about going to the Old Thrasher's Reunion at Mt.

Pleasant this Sunday? Have you ever been?"

John nodded. "Jah, when I was small my parents hired a driver to take us."

"I know the kids would love seeing all the exhibits -- the machinery and horses. It starts Thursday but coming up is the in between Sunday so I thought instead of visiting anyone, we could go to Mt. Pleasant," Hal suggested.

"Sunday is only a few days away. This is maybe too short a notice for me to find someone to drive us," John said, debating whether to say yes.

"We could take my car. I'll drive," suggested Hal offhandedly.

John lifted an eyebrow in annoyance. "Hal, you know better than that. You are not to drive your car anymore."

"What would it hurt this one time? I still drive my car to work in Wickenburg, and no one has said anything. Sunday we would be a two hour drive away from home. No one will know that we went anywhere in the car or how we got to Mt. Pleasant if they knew we were gone," Hal argued.

"I would know," John said shortly.

"Yes, but I haven't been told yet by the bishop that I have to get rid of the car. Technically, I should be able to still use it, shouldn't I?" She asked.

"I don't think so. Now that you are Plain you must obey the Ordnund laws. It seems to me you must do as the laws say without being told so by the bishop. Let me think about this matter," John said.

"Just keep in mind, Margaret told me I was getting too serious about being Amish. I should lighten up. This trip to Mt. Pleasant seemed like a good way to do it," Hal informed him.

John gave her a weak smile. "Margaret said you needed to lighten up? Perhaps, she is right, but I think you will catch on to your lot in this family and the community in due time."

"Thanks for the confidence in me, John Lapp," Hal said, patting his hand.

The next morning, John came in the kitchen while Hal was alone. "All right. We will go to Mt. Pleasant in your car, but please do not ask to drive us anywhere else after this. I am afraid this is not the right thing to do. The Ordnund is set against such things."

"I won't ask again. At least not unless the bishop says it is all right to use my car," agreed Hal.

"That is not going to happen. You should face it," John said exasperated. "I'm telling you Plain people can not drive a car according to the Ordnund. You really should get rid of the car so you ---- er we are not tempted anymore."

"I don't want to face that yet. Give me time to get used to the idea of not having a car," Hal pleaded. "Now let's tell the kids what we're doing on Sunday."

Sunday morning by daybreak they were packed in the car and on the long drive east of them. The children enjoyed the ride and the scenery. There was plenty of chatter in the back seat as they pointed out farm sights that interested them on the way. A John Deere tractor crossed a hayfield, pulling a rake that bunched up hay into windrows. Cattle herds, goat herds and various colors of horses speckled the hillside pastures.

When the Lapps arrived at the Mt. Pleasant city limits, Hal followed the signs along the streets to the Old Thrasher Reunion grounds. A man in the driveway of a parking lot a block from the ground's entry way motioned Hal in. Another man pointed to an empty space on the end of the row of cars, facing the sidewalk. Hal maneuvered the car into the parking spot.

They walked along the sidewalk and stopped at the crosswalk that led to the ground's entrance. Two policemen stood in the middle of the street, directing the traffic and pedestrians. One held his hand up to stop the Lapp family at the cross walk. He waved his arm to keep traffic moving slowly by. Finally, he held his hand up to stop the cars and motioned for the family to cross the street.

Ahead of them was the small building with a sign that indicated it was the ticket booth above the open window. Hal asked for tickets for five people. At the corner of the building, a man put a colored paper band on their wrists to show they had the right to be on the grounds and could come and go for the day.

Hal stopped at a visitor center not far behind the entrance. She bought a program book that was good for the whole Old Thrasher Reunion. Now they would know the where and when information for all the demonstrations.

"Each demonstration is at a certain time. Let's see." Hal ran her finger down the list of times. "It is 10:30 now. There's a talk about old cars in the Antique Car Building about the 1909 Stanley Steamer," Hal read and added, "Whatever that is."

"Any discussions for Plain people about antique horses?" John said, grinning at her.

The children giggled.

Hal skimmed over the pages. "Very funny. I'm afraid not. Someone is telling how the boiler and cylinder on a steam engine works. West of the tractor collection is a demonstration on threshing wheat and baling straw."

"That sounds interesting," Noah said, and Daniel agreed.

"I'd like to look at the items for sale in the buildings of exhibits and crafts over there," Hal said, pointing at the long buildings ahead of them.

Emma said to Hal, "I will go with the boys. You and Daed look around."

"Are you sure, Emma?" John said.

"Jah," she answered.

"Then I will go with Hal. We should meet up by lunch time at the gate entrance so we can eat together," John planned.

John and Hal walked through the first long building filled with tables of crafts. They dodged around people and rented golf carts driven by people who had trouble walking. As they strolled to the next building, they listened to gospel music as a band played in the family tent.

Hal didn't get excited until she spotted a bread pail in a tent full of old items. "That looks like the perfect birthday gift for Emma," she exclaimed.

John slanted his head toward his shoulder. "What is it?"

"The price tag says this is a bread pail. See the crank on the

100

side and the paddles in the bottom. The pail beats the bread," Hal explained.

John chuckled, "I think bread gets kneaded. Not beat."

"Fine then, but all Emma has to do is put the dough in and turn the crank. The paddles do all the work," Hal told him.

"Not all the work if Emma is turning the crank," John said in good humor.

Hal picked the pail up and looked it all over. "You know what I mean. This galvanized pail looks brand new. It should be worth the price."

"Maybe the fact that it looks new should tell you something," John surmised.

"What?"

"That the pail didn't work for what it was intended so that is why no one else has bought it."

"In that case, it won't go to waste at our house if it won't work for bread making. You can figure out how to take the paddles and crank out. Emma can water her chickens with it," retorted Hal. She picked the pail up and made her way around the line of people to the counter.

With so many exhibits on the vast grounds, it was hard to get through everything going on. They walked though the rows of old tractors which took awhile since this exhibit interested John. Hal tried to keep him on track to come out at a line of booths with canvas overhangs for shade.

About half way along the booths, Hal stopped and pointed excitedly. "John, that's interesting."

He looked doubtful. "An old machinery seat on an old painted milk can? Why is it interesting?"

"Will you look past what it is and think what it could be?" Hal complained.

"All right, Hal, I give up. What can it be?"

"An incentive to get the boys to fish in the pond more for the fun of it. This can be our winner's fishing throne," Hal decided.

John caught the tag flopping in the wind and groaned, "For that price, it should have a place at our table."

Hal brightened up.

"I was just teasing," John said quickly.

"I want one of those milk cans. The bright blue one I think with the red seat. It would be so good to get the boys to think of the pond as a place of enjoyment again instead of conjuring up sad memories. I'll buy it, but it's heavy. You carry it back to the car for me, please." Hal took the pail from him.

"Using this seat will not take away the bad memories the kids have about the pond," John told her.

"I know that, but I'm hoping maybe the seat will make new and better memories," Hal said.

"Maybe so but don't expect the boys memories about fishing in the pond to be any better as long as their sister, Emma, catches the most fish. She will probably be the one sitting on the seat most of the time," John predicted.

"So be it." Hal said, not about to change her mind.

The milk can seat dangled from his hand as John shook his head all the way through the entry gate. Hal walked along beside him, holding on to the bread pail. She thought this was a great outing for the Lapp family, and she was pleased with her great buys.

Since it was near noon, Emma and the boys made their way to the entrance. Noah pointed as he spotted their parents in the distance, headed along the sidewalk toward the car. He frowned as he asked, "What are they carrying?"

"Looks like Daed has a milk can, and Mama Hal has a milk pail," Daniel guessed, squinting to get a better look. "Does this mean we are going back to milking cows by hand?"

"Ach, I hope not," Noah retorted.

"Ach, nah," cried Emma softly, covering her cheeks with her hands.

"I am glad to see you agree that we should not go back to the old way of milking, my schwestern," Noah said, smiling at her concern.

"That is not what is worrying me," Emma said abruptly.

"Was ist letz?" Noah asked.

"Turn around to face this way quickly, and I will tell you what is the matter," Emma said urgently. Grabbing both boys by their shoulders, she swung them around so they faced a shelter house with pony rides for young children.

"What is wrong with you?" Noah repeated tersely.

"Stella and Moses Strutt are standing by the visitor center booth. They are staring at Hallie and Daed. I do not want Stella to see us and come over here," Emma hissed.

Noah looked over his shoulder. "Uh oh! Emma, she is watching Daed open the trunk on Mama Hal's car."

Emma looked back. Stella had moved and was now leaning on the grounds fence. With her husband beside her, she had a hand shading her eyes and was standing in a wide legged stance. A look of discovery was on her face.

"I think we're in big trouble," Emma predicted. "We must tell Daed and Hallie."

"Maybe not," Daniel replied. "We can not be sure Stella Strutt will do anything."

"Daniel is right," Noah reasoned. "We are having fun. We are already here. We should just not say anything about seeing Stella. What harm is there in our being here if it is a place that Stella Strutt comes to see. Why should we leave early because of her?"

"It is not that. It is the fact that Hallie drove her car, Noah," Emma explained frankly.

"Still maybe this will turn out all right. Why spoil the day?" Noah reasoned.

"You are probably right," Emma agreed although she looked doubtful. "Quick, get out of sight until Stella and Moses move on."

"I hope that is before Daed and Mama Hal run into them," Noah said as they took shelter behind the public restrooms.

When an a man on the loud speaker listed the name of church tents furnishings lunch, Stella and Moses turned from the fence and disappeared into the crowd. The children edged back to the entrance in time to meet Hal and John by the ticket booth, getting their wrist bands checked. Hal stopped to checked her guide book for places to eat and what was happening next. "There is the Cavalcade of Power parade. We

103

could watch all the steam engines start up and parade around the grandstands. After that, we can pick one of the tents to eat in."

Emma readily agreed with that plan. If they picked the same place to eat as the Strutts, maybe the couple would have finished eating and be gone by the time they got in the lunch line.

That afternoon, the Lapp family visited the North Village. John ushered his children past the Golden Slipper Saloon as fast as he could. He'd heard the loud music from down the block and the feisty singing. He took a quick peek over the bat wing doors at the scantily dressed women, in short black and red skirts, doing a cancan dance. One glance at the black fishnet stockings on bare legs caused John to avert his eyes. He certainly didn't want his children to see the dancers.

Hearing the boastful challenges in the middle of the street, they stopped to watch the gunslingers American West Show. That was fun. The blustering bank robbers argued with the sheriff and his deputies until the law was forced to kill all the bank robbers in a shootout.

School was in session at West Pleasant Lawn School at the end of the block. Anyone could come into the one room school house for the spelling bee. Hal tried to talk Emma into trying, but she refused.

At two that afternoon, they watched a horse powered saw mill in action, splitting a large log into boards. Then they walked through the RV park to the pioneer village. The log cabin, one room school house in session, and a barn with cows, ducks and chickens was fun to see. Everything helped them imagine what it was like in the 1850's. Hal bought each of them a large cup of ice tea at the concession stand before they watched the blacksmith at work. Finally, they looked through a wood work shop. Noah and Daniel really showed an interest in watching the carpenters when they made dovetail ends on a drawer to put it together without nails. At the log barn, Emma got a kick out of watching two small English girls trying to see under a brood hen. When the hen finally moved over, four fuzzy yellow chicks were exposed. One of the little girls pointed out the chicks had their beaks open, panting.

The man in charge of the barn said, "This is a hot day. The chicks are too warm."

"I'd be too warm too if I had to sit under a mother with that heavy coat on," replied the girl.

That remark tickled Emma.

After awhile, the family headed back to the main grounds. John gave the kids money to buy each of them a bag of popcorn. They got in the long line. All the time, Emma kept a watchful eye around her, hoping against hope that Stella Strutt had tired of all the walking and went home.

At four o'clock, Hal read off the list of events. "Some of these are a repeat of the morning shows."

John said, "I think we should head for home. It will be after milk time when we get there."

"I think you're right," Hal said. "My feet are tired. I feel like I've walked miles today."

"That is because you have, Mama Hal," Daniel chirped.

Chapter 12

The routine changed for the Lapp family after the first of September. As soon as chores were done and breakfast was over, Noah harnessed one of the horses to the buggy. The boys left for school.

The house was so quiet, it took a few days for Hal to get used to the boys not coming in and out all day. She even missed Daniel slamming a door.

On Saturday morning in mid September, Hal helped the children gather in the smaller pie pumpkins from the edge of the cornfield. They stacked the bounty at the end of the driveway. In a couple weeks, the large Jack O Lantern pumpkins would turn orange in time for Halloween sales. Emma made a For Sale Sign with the line No Sunday Sales on it. When Hal asked about that, Emma said it didn't hurt to remind English people that Plain people do not do business on Sunday ever.

That was the day before Emma's birthday. Right after lunch, Hal talked Emma and the boys into going fishing in the pond. She didn't have to do much talking to persuade them after she got the milk can seat out of the car trunk. Hal explained her idea to the children. The first one to catch a fish could sit on the seat until the next one caught a fish. Noah carried the milk can seat to the pond bank while Daniel went after the shovel to dig worms. Emma took along a can for the worms and the poles. Farmers were thankful for the dry weather now that harvest was in full swing but that meant nightcrawlers were down deep in the earth so the smaller worms would have to do.

Hal watched until the kids were out of sight behind the barn on their way to the pond. She managed to convince the gentlest horse, Ben, to come to her by bribing him with a carrot. The over friendly mare, Molly, horned in and tried to take the carrot away. Hal had learned to be firm with her ever since Molly pushed her into the pond. At least, being firm worked for Hal while she was on one side the fence and Molly was on the other.

She hitched Ben up to the carriage by herself. She was quite proud of the feat even though it took her awhile. Hal had the feeling Ben was as nervous as she was. After all, she hadn't been out alone with him or driven him since her scream frightened him into a run for his life.

When Hal snapped the lines on his back, Ben moved fast enough to blur the ground under his hooves, causing the carriage to creak. Guess he was ready for a run, but she wasn't. Hal held back on the lines to get the horse to slow down to a slow trot so she could enjoy the scenery. A gust of wind blew through the open door, whipping the fringes of hair sticking out from under her prayer cap. Rustling orange, yellow and crimson leaves cascaded across the road in front of Ben. Afraid the horse might bolt, Hal held her breath for a moment. She made sure she had a tight grip on the lines and was grateful Ben wasn't spooked by the leaves.

It was evident that the country roads all looked alike if a city woman didn't know one farmer's house from another. Hal had only been on the road to the Weber sisters that one time. It would be easy to turn the wrong way and get lost. She figured she'd just have to stop at a farm house and ask for directions if she needed help. She decided John should take her out for a few buggy rides when he had time so she'd be familiar with where her neighbors lived. She really did need to know the country roads around their farm. That would help her find someone faster who needed her nursing help.

Hal was glad when she found the right road. She knew she was going the right direction when she came to the branch running across the road. She slowed Ben down and waited for the horse to test the cold water with his front hooves and decide on his on to wade across to the road.

Just ahead of her was the Weber house. Hal parked and went to the door. When Esther answered her knock, she explained she was there to pick up Emma's birthday cake.

The ladies asked Hal to stay and visit awhile, but she told them she had to hurry home. She wanted to hide the cake before Emma came back from fishing with the boys. She was determined to surprise Emma.

The next day was the in between Sunday. That was fortunate because of the supper get together Hal had planned to celebrate Emma's birthday. She smiled to herself with that thought. Being glad for an in between Sunday so she'd get out of going to church was another one of those English transgressions she had to think and not say out loud.

That morning, Hal wished Emma a Happy Birthday when she came into the kitchen. At breakfast, she announced formally, "We are having a birthday supper in honor of Emma's birthday tonight. You are all invited."

"That is nice of you to invite us since we live here," John said, smiling at her.

The boys giggled.

Hal waved her hand at them. "You know what I meant. The Yoders and Margaret are coming for supper. We're having company."

John nodded and asked, "The boys and me are going over to Samuel Nisely's to look at his new colt this afternoon. Either one of you women want to go?"

"I think I better stay here and help Hallie," Emma said.

"I can't go this time. I have lots to do today to get ready for this party. Next time you go visit Roseanna and Samuel I'll go if that is all right. Don't stay too long so you get chores done on time. We want to be ready to eat supper when the Yoders get here," Hal warned.

John and the boys came home later that afternoon and went right to the barn to do the chores. A little later, the Yoder buggy pulled in the driveway and parked in front of the house. John came from the barn to greet them. Luke and the boys went into the barn with John. The women and the girls headed to the house. Hal noticed Josh was with them. The young man strutted along beside the other boys. She knew it was wrong of her to leave the young man out if she was really sincere about practicing her Amish ways. That hadn't kept Hal from hoping he wouldn't come with the Yoders to this special occasion.

Soon the women were busy chatting and putting the finishing touches on supper. What Hal was too busy to see before the milking was done was the buggy that pulled up by the barn. Bishop Bontrager and Deacon Enos Yutzy climbed down and disappeared into the barn. Looking way too serious, they nodded at Luke Yoder, leaning against the barn wall.

Elton said in a staid manner, "Preacher Yoder, we are all together at last."

"Jah, we are. This is the right time to have our meeting. I will get John," Luke said solemnly. He turned toward the milking parlor and walked past the boys. Noah was wiping a cow's bag with the iodine solution. Levi was sliding a full scoop shovel toward the end of the gutter. Daniel held the milking cups under a cow's bag and released them as they sucked up the teats. Josh stood, hands in his pockets, relaxed against the barn wall with no intention of helping. Luke tapped John on the shoulder as he took milking cups off a cow. Rather than yell above the generator rumble, Luke pointed toward the ministers by the door. John straightened up and spotted the men. Luke motioned for Josh to take over. The young man reluctantly unfolded from against the wall and sauntered over.

John handed Josh the milking cups and went to greet the minister and the deacon. "Wilcom, Elton and Enos. What brings you here? Coming to Emma's birthday party?"

"Nah," the bishop said, looking apprehensive.

"We want to have a private talk with you, John," Enos said reluctantly.

"It looks serious. Come away from the noise." John led the way down the alley between the stalls to the far end of the barn so they could talk without shouting. "Now what can I do for you?"

"This is official church business." Elton cleared his throat before he finished. "Bruder Lapp, we all realize there are certain temptations for all of us. Always ----," his voice trailed off as he licked his lips and studied his shoes.

Enos stroked his beard as he continued, "What Eldon is trying to say is we have been made aware ----." He looked over John's head at a cobweb and tried to find the words.

"Was ist letz?" John asked point blank.

With a somber expression, Preacher Luke Yoder finished with, "John, give us time to explain what is the matter. These gute men are finding this a hard meeting to have with you, because we have all always been gute friends. What they want to say is, we have been told you were tempted and broke one of the rules of the Ordnund."

"Which one?" John asked, but he knew before he had to be told.

"No riding in a car driven by a Plain person," the bishop got out. "Stella Strutt has been to see me. She says she saw you at Mt. Pleasant with your family. She says you went there in Nurse Hal's car. Tell me, did someone else go along and drive the car for you? That would make a big difference."

"Ach, nah! I can not tell you that," John said, wiping his sweaty forehead with his shirt sleeve. "Hal drove. I knew it was wrong when we went. I tried to talk her out of driving, but I was weak and as you say tempted by my wife. I have anguished over it ever since. I do not like the guilty feeling, knowing that I sinned against the church. I am so very sorry that I was weak."

Bishop Bontrager looked relieved. He nodded at the deacon and then Preacher Yoder. "If the two of you are satisfied, I am, too. We all know John Lapp. He has never been one to go against Ordnund rules before. I accept his admission of guilt and his willingness to not sin in this manner again. I say we should let him move on and put this in the past."

Both the deacon and Minister Yoder nodded that they agreed.

"One other thing, John," the bishop began and grimaced,

reluctant to bring the matter up. "How much does Nurse Hal use her cell phone?"

John shook his head slowly, wondering where this question came from. If he had to guess, he'd say from Stella Strutt. "Hal never uses that phone. She has it laid away somewhere in the clinic."

"That is gute, but perhaps it would be better to throw the phone away to prevent more temptation on Nurse Hal's part," the bishop suggested strongly.

"By now, the battery has probably run down. She has no way to recharge it here," John said.

"We will need to talk to her about these modern conveniences. Can you please tell her Deacon Yutzy, Preacher Yoder and myself want to see her at my house for a meeting at seven tomorrow night? We have to tell her she has to make her things right with the church by giving up the car and phone," the bishop said gravely.

"I will tell her and come with her to the meeting," John said.

"We will let you get back to your chores now so you can get in the house for supper and Emma's birthday party," the deacon said, holding out his hand to shake with John. "Have a good evening, Bruder Lapp."

John stared after Bontrager and Yutzy as they left the barn. Luke put his hand on John's shoulder. "I am sorry this had to happened. I would rather have been anywhere else than here this moment, my friend."

"So would those two men who I know are my friends. It is not your fault that this happened. I strayed from the Ordnund. I have admitted it. If I am forgiven by the church, it is a big relief to me. I have felt such a weight because of my sin," John told him.

"You are forgiven, but you realize the bishop has given you a warning with this forgiveness. If you are caught another time in Hal's car with her driving, you will be called to a member meeting to make your things right. The punishment will be worse next time," Luke warned.

"I know. I have learned my lesson," John vowed. "Now if I

could only figure out a way to talk Hal into getting rid of that car."

When John and Luke came to the house, Hal told them to sit down and visit for a few minutes until supper was ready. She thought the men looked troubled about something, but she didn't have time to let the matter more than flicker in and out of her mind. Perhaps, John was a little taken aback by all the attention she was putting on Emma's birthday. After all, it was not the Plain way to fuss over anyone, but birthdays were celebrated. Margaret had told her that much. Not that this party was much of a fuss compared to the birthday parties that English children have.

Emma deserved attention once in awhile even if it was just once a year on her birthday. She had worked so hard for years to keep house for the family and take care of everyone. It was time she had some fun.

When Noah and Daniel came inside following them was Levi, Mark and Josh.

Luke said to Hal, "We brought Josh along with us tonight."

The young man nodded glumly at Hal. His probing squint eyed stare made her feel as if he could see through her and realize she disliked him. Maybe he was holding a grudge from the afternoon of her wedding when she made sure Levi's date for supper and the singing was Emma. She sure spoiled that young man's plans. Now she thought she knew why John seemed unhappy. He had to notice how Josh acted around Emma. Though the girl didn't seem to see a difference between Levi and Josh, Hal didn't like the way Josh looked the girl up and down in an appraising manner as if Emma was a prize heifer. She didn't like that curling lip smile he used on the girl that was closer to a sneer. If she hadn't known better, she'd think Josh might be trying to imitate Elvis Presley.

While Margaret and Linda finished helping Hal in the kitchen, the girls went with the boys out to the front porch. Hal glanced out the open window ever little bit, wondering what Plain young people talked about. Emma sat between Levi and Josh on the steps with Jenny on the other side of Levi. They talked so softly Hal couldn't pick up what they said. Noah and Daniel stretched out on the grass by the base of the steps and picked at Rose. The eight year old girl usually wanted to get their attention, but at that moment, she was more interested in trying to catch Buttercat. The yellow barn cat heard talking and joined the children, looking for a little attention of his own. He wrapped himself around Rose's legs. The big cat's tail twittered in the giggling girl's face when she bent to pick him up. Buttercat proved to be too heavy for her. He wiggled to get away. She lost her grasp and dropped him. The cat skittered back to the barn to hide. Rose plopped down by the boys and complained about their unfriendly cat.

The young people's chatter and laughter floated in through the open window. That eased Hal's mind some. Emma was having a good time on her birthday with Plain folks her own age. That was the plan, and it was working.

That evening after supper, Emma was truly surprised when Hal came out of the pantry carrying the cake decorated with her name, Happy Birthday and 16 blazing blue candles. "That is such a pretty cake. You made that all by yourself, Hallie?" Emma sounded impressed.

"I wish I could say yes."

"But you shouldn't," John warned, his eyes wondering around the people in the room as a sign she needed to remain truthful.

"All right. Truthfully, Emma, the Weber sisters made it for me," admitted Hal.

"It is the thought that counts," said Emma solemnly. "We know it will be a gute cake if the Weber sisters made it."

"That's an off handed compliment if I ever heard one, but you're right. Better the cake came from them than me," Hal said as she knelt in front of the cupboard the water bucket sat on. She brought out a tissue wrapped gift while John, Luke and Noah slipped out of the kitchen. "This is from me," Hal said, setting the gift on the table.

"I am sure if you tried to make a cake it would taste as gute as this one," Emma amended as she unwrapped the tin bucket

113

with the paddle. She asked, "What is it?"

"A bread kneading bucket. Your father isn't so sure it will work so if it doesn't, you can use the bucket for watering the chickens or something," said Hal, her voice trailing off.

"Hallie, denke. It is the thoughtfulness that counts," Emma repeated, grinning.

Noah, acting as door opener, held the back door while John and Luke carried in a large birthday gift.

"A hope chest. Just what I wished I would get, Daed," Emma cried. She jumped up and came around the table to inspect the chest. It had a rounded top, and at one time was probably a streamer trunk used for travel. She ran her hand over the top of the glistening wood between the bronze bands. "This looks just like Mama's."

"It is your mother's, Emma," said Hal. "Your father and I talked about getting you a new one, but we thought you should have Diane's. Perhaps that would be more special. Your father put a new finish on it so it would look like new."

Emma teared up as she patted the chest. "You are right. To have something that was my mother's is very special. It was not only her chest. It belonged to her mother. Maybe farther back then that, it belonged to other grandmothers."

"May we be the first to put something in the hope chest." Margaret produced a gift she had hid under her apron. "Here is an offering from the Yoder family."

Emma unwrapped a pair of cotton, purple pillow cases. "Voonderball gute, denke for being so thoughtful," she exclaimed. She opened the lid of the chest and laid the pillow cases on the bottom.

Hal pulled another gift out from the cupboard. "This afternoon, I found this package in the mailbox with your name on it," she said excitedly.

"Who is it from?"

"My mom and dad. I thought I should hide it until the party. Open it. Let's see what they sent you for your birthday," Hal said, sounding as excited as Emma.

Emma cut the packing tape on the box lid and pulled back

the flaps. She found a set of seven dish towels, each with a different fruit or vegetable and the day of the week embroidered on the end. A birthday card fell out of the middle of the stack. Inside the card was a note that said, "Have a really Happy Sweet Sixteen birthday and add these dish towels to your hope chest from your grandparents. Love Dawdi and Mammi."

"Look at all the embroidery work Mammi did to make these dish towels so special," Emma exclaimed. After she placed the dishtowels beside the pillow cases, she mused, "Now if we could just get the hope chest back up those stairs, I would like it put in my room."

Luke said to John, "I can help with that job." The men picked it up and left the room.

Chapter 13

After the company left that evening, Emma plopped down in a chair at the table by Hal. "Where did you find that unusual bread kneading pail?"

"At the Old Thrasher's Reunion. Your father helped me get the pail and the milk can for the boys back to the car while you were sightseeing." Emma's face turned blotchy as she bit her bottom lip. "Emma, is everything all right?"

The girl took a deep breath. "Jah, What could be wrong? Guess I am just tired. Ach, but I have had a voonderball gute birthday, Hallie," Emma exclaimed, kissing Hal on the cheek. Looking away, she paused.

"What is it?" Hal asked.

"Such a surprise to get a gift from Mammi and Dawdi. How did your folks know that I would be getting a hope chest for my birthday?"

"Actually the idea was Mom's. While she was here, she saw your mother's chest and admired the workmanship on it. She said someday we should give you Diane's hope chest. She said it would mean more to you than it would to me just sitting in a corner of the bedroom collecting dust. Besides, she knew I was getting a new hope chest at the wedding. When your daed told me about your approaching birthday, I wrote Mom and told her now was the time to send you something to put in a hope chest. Our gift was your mother's hope chest, because John said a hope chest is what Plain girls get on their sixteenth birthday."

"I am glad Mammi and you thought to give me such a special gift," Emma said.

After the evening prayer, Emma announced to them all,

"Josh has asked me to the singing Sunday evening at Metta Yutzy's house."

"Do you want to go?" John asked.

"Jah. Josh is new in the neighborhood. He thought me going with him would be a gute way to get acquainted with people our age," Emma said.

"*He* thought so, did he? Margaret told me Josh is eighteen," Hal offered, looking uneasy.

John nodded. He understood her meaning. Eighteen was not that much older than Emma, but that young man did not have a very pleasing personality. He paused to lay his bible back on the bookshelf before he said to Emma, "If that is what you want to do it is all right with me."

"That is gute. I think I need to get into bed. I am tired," Emma said.

The boys played checkers for awhile. Finally, John looked at Hal as he said, "Boys, put the checkers away and go to bed."

"Daed, I am win----," Daniel started to complain.

"I think it is time to call it a night now," John said firmly.

Hal had an uneasy feeling as she watched John's gloomy face. It was the same feeling she had when he came in from chores. Something was wrong. From his grave look and sound of his voice, she was certain she wasn't going to like knowing what it was. After the boys disappeared upstairs, he clasped his hands together in his lap and studied Hal.

She said in a low voice, "John, I know something is wrong. Just tell me. Are you upset that I gave Emma a birthday party?"

"Ach, nah. This has been *almost* a voonderball gute evening," he said dryly.

"Almost, but not completely good. Is it about that boy, Josh? Quite honestly, I didn't like the idea of Emma going anywhere with him before we get to know him better. I've had a bad feeling about him ever since the first time I met him," Hal admitted.

"Now who is being overly protective?" John said with a gleeless smile on his face.

"It's my women's instinct about men that tells me that boy is no good. Trust me," Hal insisted.

"I do, and I feel the same way, but I have to trust Emma to make gute decisions now that she has come of age to go out with boys. Right now she is curious about this one, because we have so few young strangers that live near us. If I protested about Josh, she would be more drawn to him. If she is allowed to see through him herself, she will be the wiser for it. It is not about Josh that I am worried right now. It is something else, and it is a worse thing at the moment for you than it is for me." John hesitated.

"You're really worrying me. What's the matter?"

John cleared his throat, suddenly looking sad and tired. "Did you see the buggy with Elton Bontrager and Enos Yutzy in it drive up by the barn at milk time?"

Hal shook her head. "No, what did they want?"

"They came to call on me about official church business. They came tonight while Luke Yoder was here. It was a meeting with church ministers. They confronted me about riding in your car when you drove to Mt. Pleasant," John said.

Hal groaned. "They found out. What did they say?"

John studied his folded hands grimly. "They questioned me and accused me of committing a sin against the Ordnund. I agreed that I was guilty."

"And?"

"They said since I was not a man to sin and break the Ordnund rules they believed me when I said I am remorseful. It had to be the bishop's decision to forgive me. He did. Deacon Yutzy and Luke agreed with him. I am forgiven in the eyes of the church unless I repeat the same temptation again. If I get caught, which is never going to happen again, I would have to go before a member meeting at church where the members decided if I am guilty as charged. If they so say, I would be disciplined severely. But as of now, this matter is over and forgotten for me."

"Oh good. You aren't in trouble anymore," Hal said with a sigh. Then she frowned. "What about the children?"

"They are not baptized in the church yet so they are not in

118

trouble. They do not have to follow the rules of the Ordnund until they are a member of the church." John took a deep breath. "It is true I am not in trouble, but you are in very much trouble yet. Elton said you have to meet him, Luke and Deacon Yutzy at his house tomorrow night at seven to discuss this matter with them," John informed her.

"I do, do I? Just like that. He didn't come to the house to ask me if I'd like to come. He commanded that I be there and had you tell me," Hal rankled.

John was irritated when he said, "The bishop has spoken. He doesn't ask when he wants to have a meeting about a church member's breaking the Ordnund rules. You must obey his order to go see him. His word is our law. Usually Elton would have talked to you personally in private, but with the birthday party tonight, he did not want to confront you in front of company. For your sake and Emma's, he wanted this to be a happy time."

"All right, I get it. I truly didn't think anyone would be the wiser about our outing. What has happened to cause us all this trouble?" Hal asked, alarmed now.

"Stella and Moses Strutt was at the Old Thrasher Reunion. Stella could not wait to get back to Elton to tell him she saw you driving your car and my family was with you," John said.

"Fudge! Of course, Stella would hurry right to Elton. She's probably trying to get even with us for Daniel's frog causing her to make a spectacle out of herself at the wedding. I'm sure she's been on her high horse ever since that day," spit Hal.

"Hal!" John arched an eyebrow.

"All right, I'm sorry I said that about Stella." Hal put her hand up in the air. "I hope to kiss a pig if I'm not sorry. It just sort of snuck out. Stella Strutt always seems to rub me the wrong way."

"That may be, but truth is we should not have went anywhere in your car. It is not Stella's fault that we broke an Ordnund law. That was our decision. Now we have both gotten in trouble for being tempted to use that car," John said ruefully.

"I am so sorry, John. I didn't think this would happen. What will Elton say to me?"

"Be prepared. He told me to tell you he is going to tell you that you have to sell the car," John said bluntly. "The moment has come that you have to face this."

"Oh," Hal groaned. "I can't imagine going to Wickenburg all winter, in the cold and snow, in the carriage to do my Home Health job. My car has a heater and gets me there faster."

"You can quit the job if you want to. You do not have to work away from home. Just take care of the clinic patients here. Soon you will have a baby to take care of which will take up your time," John suggested.

Hal's voice cracked. "I might agree if more Plain people consented to come to the clinic so I could stay busy. I really enjoy being a nurse. It's what I went to school to do. I'm good at it, and I hate to give up my job. What am I going to do?"

John paused for a moment. "Have you ever thought about taking a lay off in the winter from the job and going back to work in the spring? That way the ride to town would be warmer and safer for you out alone while you drive the buggy."

"I've never heard of anyone else that ever does that," Hal declared.

"Barb is a gute friend. She would understand. Gute nurses are hard to come by and keep. She might consent to do this for you just so she has your job filled part of the time."

"All right, I'll talk to Barb to see if she's agreeable to that. Otherwise, if I have to I'll have to drive Ben all winter," Hal said reluctantly.

"There's one more thing. Bishop Bontrager wants you to throw away that cell phone."

"Throw away my cell phone?"

"Doing these things are the only way to be forgiven by our church," John insisted.

"Will that be the end of this if I do as I'm asked?"

"Jah, you have to tell the ministers you are guilty, and you will repent. To be forgiven like they did me, you will have to look and act like you mean what you say. We can only pray that will be enough. The punishment may be worse for you," John explained earnestly.

Hal looked puzzled. "I don't understand. All you had to do was say you were sorry out in the barn, and they forgave you. Why wouldn't that be enough for me tomorrow night at Elton and Jane's house?"

"I was just a passenger. You were the Plain person driving the car. That is a worse offense than my riding in it," justified John.

Hal studied John's face. "So you really don't know what will happen to me?"

"Believe me, it did not feel gute when I was accused of being tempted by my new wife *who's name should have been Eve* even though I knew I was guilty. The first offense is usually forgiven if the person says they are guilty. If the offense continues that is when Plain folks have to make our things right in front of the other church members.

In your case if the bishop decides it needs to be, he will tell you to make sure you are at a member meeting at the next Gemeesunndaag. The meeting happens right after the church service. You have to confess you are guilty in front of all the congregation. I told him I will come with you tomorrow night so you do not have to face him and the other two alone."

"Oh dear, now I'm so very sorry I dragged you into this," Hal said, tears in her eyes. "They won't decided to excommunicate me, will they? I just became Amish and have a lot to learn. Can't they take that into account this one time?"

"Excommunication is for those that continue to sin. That would be too harsh a punishment for the first time. That will not happen. Once you are Amish, you are supposed to know right from wrong, but usually you will be given chances to make your things right as long as you do not continue to sin. We will have to take whatever Elton decides is your punishment this time and live with it. We know we cannot make the same mistake again, and we move on. That is all we can do," John said stoically. He held out his hand to help Hal up. "Now we need our rest."

121

Chapter 14

The next morning when Hal woke up, she realized her heart wasn't in going to work. She didn't even feel like getting out of bed. She remembered when John got up. That had been awhile ago. She smelled bacon cooking. Emma was making breakfast. Smells from the kitchen wafting up the stairs was enough to make her stomach pitch and roll. She'd be all too happy to be rid of morning sickness. A feeling of guilt came over her for lying in bed while Emma worked. Hal made herself get out of bed.

Sunlight coming through the window made the kitchen cheery, but that didn't had much affect on Emma's disposition. As she watched the girl from the doorway, Hal decided it wouldn't help to say good morning. Emma kneaded the bread dough with a fervor. For what the girl was putting the dough through, Hal was sure this one time the term beat was more accurate.

On Emma's face was a look that Hal seldom saw except when the girl was trying to defend her for some reason. "I take it your father told you what is in store for me tonight," Hal blurted out.

"Jah, he did." Emma socked the bread hard with her fist.

"I'd ask how come you're aren't using the bread pail I got you but looks to me like you need to take your anger out on something," Hal said. "Maybe beating on that bread dough will make you feel better, but I doubt it."

"When I think about Stella Strutt nothing makes me feel better. I knew she was going to be trouble that day."

Hal studied her. "You knew before hand that Stella would

have a reason to go to the bishop? That's why you looked so flustered when I brought up The Old Thrasher Reunion last night."

Emma got a I've been busted look on her face. "I should have said something before this. Hallie, the boys and me saw Stella and Moses watching Daed and you go to your car with the things you bought. We talked about telling you and decided not to worry you. We were having so much fun. It might make Daed want to leave right away. Worse, we did not want him getting mad at you. We hoped Stella would be silent for once in her life." Emma turned the bowl over on the floured counter and slapped the bottom hard. When she lifted the bowl, the glossy ball of dough looked, if anything, better for its beating.

Hal rushed over to her. "Emma, listen to me. What I did was wrong. I shouldn't have talked your father into letting all of us ride in my car. I thought we wouldn't get caught, but we did. Now I have to pay for that mistake by talking to the ministers tonight. So be it. Rules are made to be kept. Isn't what's happening to me what any of you have to do if you do something wrong?"

"Members do. Jah," said Emma, slowly.

"Just remember it was you that said we should turn the other cheek as far as Stella is concerned. She couldn't cause us trouble like this if I hadn't given her a reason. Isn't that right?"

"Jah, Hallie." Emma's warring attitude started to deflate.

"I very much want to be apart of this community and this family. I must follow the Ordnund like other church members. Let me learn from my mistakes and take my punishment. That is the way it should be," Hal told her.

"That is as it should be," Emma repeated softly as she wiped a tear away with her hand and left a streak of flour on her cheek.

"Did your father tell you any other news? Good news?"

Emma paused to think. "Nah, I do not remember anything gute."

"Next year, you're going to have a baby brother or sister. I hope that's all right," Hal shared tentatively.

"Really! Oh, Hallie, that is voonderball news. Wait until the boys here this." Emma danced around the table and stopped to give Hallie a hug.

That was the response Hal hoped for. Now Emma was feeling better. "You want to help me tell them when we get the right moment?" Hal asked.

"Jah, we are having a baby. Can we tell everyone?"

"One thing at a time. Let's wait until after tonight when I'm through with my punishment. Once that is out of the way, you can tell anyone you want to," Hal assured her.

That afternoon, Hal had to go into Wickenburg to visit her clients for the Home Health Department. She walked across the yard to her car and hesitated as she reached to open the door. She probably shouldn't drive the car, but she reasoned she'd be late if she hooked up Ben and drove the buggy to town.

Mrs. Johnson would be on the phone to Barb and maybe even call her daughter who would call Barb to complain that Hal was late. The last thing she needed was Barb irritated with her when she was about to ask for a winter layoff. Besides, the air was chipper with a hint of fall. She just couldn't face seeing her breath all the way to Wickenburg. At least not until she had the car taken away from her officially. Her punishment wasn't until tonight so why not drive the car one last time.

She only had two clients, Mrs. Johnson and Mrs. Wagoner, that she checked on once a week. After she finished with her clients, she headed home. She had felt dread all day, dragging her down. Guilt ate at her as she worried about what she should do. It was her fault John got into trouble with Bishop Bontrager and the other church officials. Maybe she could convince Elton that riding in the car was all her idea. He and the church members shouldn't think badly of John. Perhaps, she could use the reasoning she hadn't realized she was causing such a sinful offense. Elton was a kind hearted man. He liked her. She hoped he'd be willing to listen.

By the time she came to the Lapp driveway, she'd convinced herself to drive on past. She'd talk to Elton alone. If she went early, she'd have that chance before John and the other

124

ministers came at seven. Maybe she could convince the bishop not to think too critical of a good man like John. She'd take the blame for what happened without John being there to protest or try to protect her. Elton could say what he had to about what was going to happen to her car and to her. If she had to sell the car, she'd do it if that got her and John out of this trouble with the church.

Hal could see the bishop sitting at the kitchen table reading his bible when Jane let her in the front door. She said, "I'm here to talk to the bishop, Jane."

"Aren't you a little early, Hal?" Jane asked. Her sad brown eyes spoke volumes.

Hal gave her a pleading look. "Yes, but I just couldn't wait any longer to resolve this."

Elton called, "Come into the kitchen, Nurse Hal." When she appeared in the doorway, he said, "Sit down with me. We need to talk."

"I know. John told me." Elton's face was more flushed than usual. She wondered if he'd gotten too much sun today or was really that upset with her. The latter was more like it. His blood pressure was probably way too high at the moment. This type of conversation about discipline with someone he liked couldn't be easy for him. Bishops didn't get paid to be the head of the church. Elton had to like what he did to help others until difficult times like these came along, and he had to dispense punishment.

Elton rubbed a hand over his chest as he frowned. "Jane is right. You are early. Deacon Yutzy and Preacher Yoder will not be here for some time." He looked worriedly toward the door. "Where is John? I thought he was going to be at this meeting, too."

"He'll be here later. I didn't tell him I was coming ahead of time to talk to you alone." Hal said honestly. "I'll go home and get him after we talk. He can come back with me at seven."

The bishop gave her a stern look. "Was that your car I heard drive up?"

"Yes, I've been in town working for the Home Health

Department this afternoon. I came from Wickenburg straight here," Hal said meekly, looking under her ducked head at the bishop. Moisture glistened on Elton's skin as the sun shone on him through the kitchen window.

"I see. John told you about Stella Strutt coming to see me," Elton said, pronouncing every word with an effort between deep breaths.

"Yes, he did. Elton, er Bishop, er oh, forgive me for interrupting, but you don't feel well. I can tell," Hal said, more concerned about him than herself at the moment. "What's wrong with you, Elton?"

"He hasn't felt well all day," declared Jane from the other room. She appeared in the door to look for herself.

"I'm just a little short of breath. It always goes away in a short time," Elton excused, waving his hand at Jane.

"Always!" Hal exclaimed. "You've had shortness of breath often?"

"Not often. Just once in awhile. Now we need to get back to the subject of your car already and while we're at it your cell phone, Hallie Lapp. I have to make a decision about this. I can not believe you are still driving your car now that you are Plain. I explained to John last night what this talk would be about. I thought he was going to tell you."

Suddenly, the bishop grimaced and gripped his chest tightly, crumbling his shirt in his hand as he doubled over. A quick, hard pain shot across his chest then eased up. Elton straightened back up in his chair, but his shoulders sagged. Hoarsely, he spoke with an effort. "Plain people do not own cars and phones for a reason. Owning a car tempts him or her to travel more. It causes Plain people to stray from our basic Christian ideals. I thought this was something that you understood when you became one of us. We talked about this before, Hal, during your lessons. I will repeat in Romans 12:2. It says 'Be not conformed to this world but be ye transformed by renewing of your mind that ye may prove what it is that is good and acceptable and perfect the will of God.' We believe and live by that and that includes you now."

126

Elton grasped his chest again and doubled over on the table, letting out a loud groan.

The nurse in Hal took over. She jumped up and ran around the table. Bishop or not, this was a very sick man. "Elton, I'm taking your pulse." She grabbed his wrist and gripped it tightly to keep him from resisting as she felt his fast, erratic pulse. At the same time, she felt his moist forehead. He was diaphoretic. Hal watch his labored breathing for a respiration count. "You are going to the hospital as fast as we can get you there."

"What is it?" Jane cried, rushing to the table.

"It's his heart," Hal told her. "Do you have aspirins?

"Jah."

"Bring me an aspirin and get a pillow to take with us." Jane disappeared toward the bedroom. Hal filled a glass with water and sat it on the table as she asked, "Elton, can you walk?"

"I think I can," he gasped.

Jane hustled back with a pillow. She laid it on the counter and reached in a cupboard, brought out a bottle and handed Elton the aspirin. The women waited for him to swallow the aspirin with water.

"Fine. Now we'll help you stand up. Give me the pillow, Jane." Hal tucked the pillow under her arm and secured her other arm under Elton's arm. "Now, Jane, take his arm. Between the two of us, we have to get him to car. He needs to get to the hospital as quick as he can."

Elton leaned heavily on the women, bobbing up and down on his weak knees. Hal was sure he didn't have much more energy left for walking. He panted as he wobbled and bumped Hal then into Jane. Any minute Hal expected the elderly man to pass out, but they couldn't rush him. All they could do was hope he made it to the car before he collapsed.

Hal was pushed into the wooden facing as they went through the outside door. Too late she heard a long grating rip. The door hook had snagged into the feather pillow. Feathers flew out of the rip. A stiff breeze came directly at them, causing a snow storm effect as white fluff scattered. Hal looked back at the mess shifting over the living room and kitchen.

"Jane, I'm so sorry," she said contritely.

As they went down the steps, Jane looked over her shoulder. "Don't worry. That is what we call a clean mess."

"One that I will clean up for you. I promise," Hal vowed. "Once we have Elton in the car could you get another pillow. This time if you carry the pillow out here it might be safer."

Elton slid into the back seat and scooted over to make room for Jane. Hal opened the driver's door and leaned over to the passenger seat. She fished her phone out of her neon green nursing bag with Life Is A Blast on the front. She hesitated just a second. She was about to commit another violation right in front of the bishop, but she reminded herself this man wasn't just the bishop. He was her friend and a very sick man that needed medical help right away. She flipped open her phone and used speed dial for 911. "This is Nurse Hallie Lapp with the Home Health Department. Send an ambulance south out of Wickenburg to meet me on the highway. I'm bringing in a heart attack patient that has been having symptoms most of the day. I'll pull over and flash my car lights when I see the ambulance coming. Tell the driver to run with sirens and have an EMT on board."

Jane got in with Elton and propped him up against the pillow. Hal closed the back door and slid behind the steering wheel. She slipped the phone in her dress pocket and fished the adapter out of her bag to put with the phone. Then she looked in the rear view mirror. "Jane, the ambulance is meeting us on the highway. You keep me posted how Elton is doing. Keep talking to him."

Jane patted Elton's claw like hand as he dug at his chest. She said in quiet concern, "Stay calm, Elton. Nurse Hal is helping us. With God's help, all will be gute. Nurse Hal knows what she is doing."

Elton muttered something to Jane. Hal made out the words car and phone. She saw Jane put a finger to her husband's lips. "Just stay calm, Elton and we will pray about this at another time. Let us take care of you first."

Hal turned onto Wickenburg highway and drove a couple

miles. A whirl of red and blue lights splashed across the windshield and her face. The whining siren grew louder as the fast moving ambulance came toward the car. She moved over and carefully pulled off onto the shoulder before she flickered her headlights off and on. The ambulance slowed down, past the car, did a U turn in the road and parked behind Hal. In no time, the crew had Elton loaded in the ambulance. Hal and Jane watched from the side of the road. The siren screamed, and lights flashed as the ambulance headed back toward the hospital.

"Come on, Jane. Get up front with me. We'll follow the ambulance," Hal said as she tossed her nursing bag into the back seat.

Jane hesitated then said in a quietly sad voice, "Nah."

Hal studied her friend.

"I must ride in back. It is our way," Jane said as she opened the back door.

"I understand," Hal told her. "Let's hurry."

At the hospital ER doors, the ambulance was already pulling out from under the canopy when Hal parked her car. The automatic doors opened with a swoosh when the women rushed close.

Bathed in the stark brightness of florescent lights, Nurse Lucy Stineford looked up from her paperwork. She smiled when she recognized Hal. "Hi. I hear you're an old married woman now."

"Yes, I am that and loving it. Which ER room did they take Elton Bontrager to?"

"Four. They're working on him now. Listen, you know the drill. You just have to wait," Lucy said, studying the obviously worried Amish woman beside Hal.

Hal nodded toward Jane. "This is the patient's wife, Jane Bontrager."

"Mrs. Bontrager, we won't know much for awhile. Go into the waiting room and take a seat. You can fill out the paper work for your husband while you wait." Lucy picked up a clipboard she'd just loaded with forms and lead the way to the row of chairs.

Hal didn't know how long they spent waiting, looking toward the exam room and trying to keep up a conversation. It had to be the better part of an hour. When Hal couldn't sit still any longer, she told Jane she'd check to see if there was an update. Hal asked Lucy, but the nurse still didn't know anything encouraging yet.

While they were talking, Hal fished her phone out of her pocket and the adapter. "Could you charge my phone for me while I'm here, Lucy?"

"Sure. Hand it over," Lucy said.

"I'll get it before I leave. Don't let me forget." Hal turned around. Jane was in the waiting room doorway, staring at the cell phone in Lucy's hand. "I suppose I'm in even bigger trouble now for using my phone and bringing Elton to the ambulance with my car," Hal admitted contritely.

Chapter 15

Jane shrugged her shoulders. "I am not sure. I do know how thankful I am that you helped try to save my husband. He did not seem too concerned to be riding with you while he was in such pain," Jane reminded her.

"I wouldn't want anything to happen to a good man like Elton. I must confess I'm not one bit sorry I got him here as quick as I did by putting him in my car," Hal said adamantly.

Jane gave her a hard look. "What was bothering him just as much was your use of that cell phone. He told John the phone should be thrown away. John said the battery had run down, and it was not usable anymore. Elton thinks John lied to him to protect you."

Hal felt her stomach lurch. She'd purposely not told John she kept her phone battery charged. Now she'd gotten him in trouble again. "Jane, John doesn't know about the phone. I never use it at home so he just assumed it didn't work. When the battery runs down, I charge it up while I'm in town, taking care of my clients. I've never intended to use it except in an emergency like this one," Hal said sincerely.

Jane agreed sadly, "Jah and this certainly was an emergency. I will explain to Elton that he was wrong about John if ----." She took a deep breath as she looked down the hallway. "When Elton is better."

A couple hours later, the ER doctor finally came out of exam room four. He headed toward Jane and Hal. They saw nurses briskly moving in and out of door four but that didn't tell them anything except that Elton must still yet alive for there to be that much activity.

The doctor nodded at Jane. Behind him was a nurse that assisted him. "Mrs. Bontrager, I'm Stan Christensen. I've been taking care of your husband. He's going to be admitted for observation and tests. I don't know exactly how long he will stay in the hospital but probably a few days."

Jane nodded and waited for more.

"He had a mild heart attack, but it could have been much worse. It's a good thing Hal got him to the ambulance as quick as she did. The EMT had a chance to work on your husband before the ambulance arrived at the hospital to help stabilize him. The thing is we still don't have his condition as stable as we'd like. That's why we're keeping him. Tomorrow we'll do the tests to see what we can do to help Mr. Bontrager. You can stay here with him tonight if you like, but you need to get your rest. It would be better for you to go home and come back in the morning. We'll take good care of him."

"I am sure you will, but I am staying," Jane said firmly.

"All right. Your husband is going to be in a double room. You can sleep on the empty bed. The nurse will take you to your husband," he said.

Jane walked along with the nurse. Hal followed. The nurse stopped at the door of Eldon's room. "He may be groggy so don't try to make him talk. He needs to stay calm and rest."

"Denke, Nurse," Jane said in a hushed voice and rushed across the room to the bed.

Elton didn't seem to know anyone was in the room. He was sleeping and breathing easy. The monitor was still hooked up to him. Air filled the blood pressure cuff on his arm and registered a new set of vitals on the screen.

Hal whispered, "Jane, he looks like he isn't in pain now. He's resting easy."

"That is gute," Jane said, trying to be positive but she was worried just the same.

"Jane." When the woman didn't seem to hear, Hal patted her on the shoulder. Jane turned. "I'm going home now that I know Elton is doing better. The nurse said not to get him excited. I might just be more than he wants to see when he wakes up. If you don't need me?"

"Nah, we will be fine. As the doctor said, Elton is in gute hands here," Jane assured her. "You need to get some rest, too."

"Promise me you'll get on that bed over there and try to get some sleep. Don't stand here hovering over Elton all night. Save that for when he's awake. If he's like most men, when he wakes up he will want lots of special attention from you. Sick men usually do."

"That is right." Jane giggled with her hand over her mouth.

Hal patted her friend's shoulder. "If you need me for anything at all tonight, call me. The nurse will have my cell phone number. Just this once, I'm going to lay my phone by my bed so I can hear it ring."

"Denke and denke for all you've done for Elton," Jane said in a hushed voice, giving Hal a hug. "Please do not worry about what Elton will do or think. He is a fair man, and I intend to have a talk with him when he feels better. I will remember to call you if I need you. Now go home."

Hal had wanted to see what she could get out of the Lucy about Elton's condition, but she wasn't at the nurse's station. Dr. Christensen was. "Exactly how bad is this heart problem for Elton Bontrager, Stan?"

"This is a man that needs to take better care of himself at his age. He needs a different diet, and I'm betting tests will show he not only needs blood pressure medicine but cholesterol pills to get him healthier. We'll know more when we get the tests done."

Hal had a mental image of her father with the same physical problems. As soon as she could, she'd have to get a letter written to him about what happened to Elton. She wanted to urge him to go to the doctor for a checkup. She heard the doctor saying to her, "Mr. Bontrager will have to take it easy for a while until we know he's out of the woods."

Hal looked sideways at him. "It's time for the corn harvest."

"I know," Stan snorted. "Saying to an Amish man that he should take it easy is like talking to a fence post. Gets the same results. It don't keep me from trying."

133

"Good for you," Hal said.

"I'm going to check on Mr. Bontrager throughout the night. That's where I'm headed now," the doctor told her.

"Home is where I'm headed. I'll be back in the morning to check on both Bontragers." Hal parted from the doctor and headed behind the nurse's station to retrieve her phone. She nodded at the janitor sloshing a mop over the shiny wax floor and walked out into the fresh night air. Taking a deep breath, she tried to rid her nostrils of the smell of antiseptics, alcohol and cleaning products which just reinforced her feeling that the Lapp family almost lost a dear friend.

It was late by the time Hal parked in front of her house. The glimmer of a lamp in the living room told her someone was still up. As she came through the door, John looked up from his bible.

"Hi," Hal said.

"Hello," he replied, giving her a concerned once over. In the dim light, it was clear John had been worried about her. Had he actually thought she might have run away rather than face the ministers tonight? A sound of annoyance crept into her husband's voice. "You are late coming home. Was ist letz?"

Hal flopped down on the couch. "Wait until you hear what is the matter. This has been just the most awful night."

"I've been wondering where you were and terrible worried. You were supposed to go with me to the bishop's meeting tonight. That is not something you can ignore," John accused.

Hal rankled at his tone. "Did you think I was hiding out to keep from going with you?"

"Jah," John answered, irritated.

"I wouldn't have done that. You should think better of me, John Lapp. I did go to the Bontrager house. It's just I wanted to get there before you did and try to get Elton not to be so mad at you," Hal confessed.

John leaned forward and rested his elbows on his knees. His tone was weary as if he was tired of trying to explain to his new wife. "He is no longer upset with me. I told you that. How did the meeting go for you?"

Hal rubbed the back of her neck. "It didn't go well at all. Before Elton got too far into what he wanted to tell me about me driving the car or using my cell phone, he had a heart attack."

"Nah!" John straightened fast like he'd been kicked by a horse.

Hal rushed on, "Yes, right at the kitchen table. Really scared Jane and me." When she saw the stricken look on John's face, she said, "Elton is doing all right for now. His vitals were better when I left the hospital. At least, he seems to have a chance to be all right according to the doctor. We have to wait for a few days to see if his heart settles down, and they are going to do tests to see what they can do to keep this from happening again. Elton will have to take several medications from now on I afraid." She leaned back limply against the couch, suddenly drained of energy. "When it happened I was afraid Jane and I weren't going to be able to get Elton in the car. He's a heavy fellow and didn't hardly have the strength to walk. Wobbled all over the place and his knees buckled with each awful chest pains."

John looked overwhelmed. "Ach nah! You telling me you took the bishop to the hospital in your car?"

"Jah." Hal saw the dismayed look on his face and felt like crying. She said in a tiny voice, "Well, not all the way. I called for the ambulance on my cell phone to meet me on the highway. Elton didn't have time to waste. He'd been feeling ill all day."

"Your cell phone still works? You used your phone to make a call in front of Elton?" John snapped.

"From Elton's vital signs, I knew we'd be too late by the time we hooked up his buggy and tried to make it to the hospital. John, you have to understand the man was having bad chest pains, a rapid, unstable heart beat and trouble breathing. I knew the sooner I got him to an ambulance the better chance he had of not dying."

John stared at her, trying to absorb what she said. "I see," he said quietly. "Go on."

"The ambulance crew had a defibrillator to shock Elton's heart if they needed it and oxygen. They could do things for Elton I couldn't. The nurse said it took awhile to get his blood pressure down and stabilize him. After the longest wait ever, the doctor came to the waiting room. He told Jane he had Elton moved to a hospital room. He's under observation. Jane wanted to spend the night with Elton. He was asleep and looked to be in no pain so I told her I'd come on home. She is to call me if he was to get worse in the night so I can go back to be with her," Hal said, rubbing her forehead to ease the nagging throb trying to defend herself had caused.

"On your cell phone Jane Bontrager will talk to you? I thought the battery had run down by now," John puzzled.

"Yes, on my cell phone. It still works just fine, denke very much. I just don't use it, but I'm leaving it in plain sight on my dresser tonight, John Lapp, so I can find it in the dark if Jane calls me," Hal said with determination. "Helping a friend is more important right now than what Plain folks think of my use of that phone. Jane is okay with this so you should be, too."

"All right." John held both hands palm up in defeat.

"Just so you know. You aren't in trouble with the bishop about the phone. I told Jane you thought the battery had run down, because you didn't know I took it to work with me to charge the battery. When Elton is feeling better, Jane said she'd explain that to him." John was boring a hole through her, but she continued, "I need to get some rest. I'll have to get up really early in the morning to go back to the Bontrager house for awhile to clean up ----," she paused and decided to change what she meant to say. "To do something for Jane. After that, I'll go to the hospital to be with Jane and Elton."

"You don't need to go to the Bontrager house."

Hal shook her head. "Oh, but I do. You don't know what happened."

"If you mean the millions of feathers all over the place, I know about that." John smiled weakly.

"You saw them?"

"Jah, when you did not come home, I went over for the

meeting at seven to see if I could defend you not showing up. I found the inside door open. Somehow, I had the idea you might have been there early when I saw feathers all over. It was the sort of thing I knew you had something to do with, but I couldn't figure out how it happened. I was really worried when I found the Bontragers not home. I did not know where to start looking for you or them. I realize emergencies happen that take you away from home when you are a nurse, but from now on, let one of us know where you are so we do not have to worry."

Hal didn't like his ultimatum. It sounded more like a command than concern. She'd just been ordered to tell him when she went anywhere, and he meant to be obeyed. This must be one of those times she was to fear the Lord, obey her husband and be the submissive wife. She knew it for what it was, but she was too tired to defend herself so she willingly let him have the last word. "I'm sorry I worried you. I'll let you know where I am from now on," she said meekly, hoping that would suffice. She had to keep in mind that John had a hard worrisome evening, too. "And about the feathers. You're right about that mess being my fault, but it was a weird accident. Jane handed me the pillow. I tucked it under my arm and held Elton up with the other arm. Between me, Jane, Elton and the pillow, the doorway wasn't wide enough. The pillow cover hung up on the screen door hook which ripped the pillow open. I don't want Jane to come home to that mess. She's going to be tired enough and needs to look after Elton. If I know her, she won't sleep a wink tonight in that hospital."

"Never mind. I came back home to get Emma to help me clean the house up. By the time, we got back Deacon Yutzy and Luke were there, looking at the feathers and wondering where the Bontragers had gone. They helped catch the feathers so it did not take so long," John explained.

"Oh, my. You all did that. Denke. I did hate to face that task in the morning by myself." She studied John's weary face and realized as worried as he had been about her, he did what he could to help at the moment. She relented about him ordering her to let him know where she was going at all times. "I can see how the sight of all those feathers in that empty house must have worried you."

"Not only that. If you ever think about having a pillow fight with me do not try it. Feathers are not that easy to catch. Just try to keep them in an old pillow case while pouring in another hand full. It was almost impossible. We felt like we were starting over each time." John got up, came over and took her hand. He pulled her off the couch. "I want you to know I am thankful you were with Elton. It was meant to be that way. I am very sure gute nurse that you are you did save his life, and I agree friends are important." He leaned down and kissed her. "Come on. We should get some sleep. In the morning, I want to go to the hospital with you. The boys can finish the milking when you are ready to leave."

The next morning, the Lapp family got an early start on chores. Emma said she'd like to go with John and Hal to the hospital. Hal was glad to have her along. Maybe it would be easier to face Elton if both John and Emma went in first so she could hide behind them.

After breakfast, Hal offered to turn the chickens loose and feed them while Emma changed dresses. She opened the hen house door. All the hens tried to come out the door at the same time. Some scooted down low and hopped out to scurry away and others flew past her head and over her shoulder.

Hal scattered handfuls of corn on the ground from a pail as the chickens flocked around her feet. They were eager to start their day and forever hungry. She wished she could be as eager as chickens were each morning. Sleep had not come easy last night. She worried about Elton and feared the phone might ring with bad news. She worried about when her punishment would finally be meted out to her now that the meeting was postponed. Would the bishop have to give her a rougher punishment because of her helping him? It wasn't going to be easy to get through each day with those thoughts hanging over her. She finally dozed off into a fitful sleep and awoke early in a glum mood with her worries still tumbling around in her mind. Not even the perky sparrows singing outside the bedroom window helped her mood.

A heavy peck on the toe of her shoe brought her back to what she was doing. She looked down and stared in disbelief at a half grown mallard with a few iridescent green feathers around his neck. He gave her a bossy quack and shook his body to ruffle his feathers up as if to say, "Pay attention! I'm back. Thought you got rid of me, didn't you?"

"Emma isn't going to be happy you showed back up, Mister. I think I'm going to let someone else tell her you returned," Hal declared. "I should warn you one of these days when you're a little bit bigger you may find yourself in the roaster pan if you keep making a nuisance out of yourself." She threw the last handful of grain among the hens.

The drake turned his back on her and pushed among the chickens, knocking them out of his way. He hurried to gobble up more than his fair share. When the corn was gone, the duck craned his neck low and searched the area around the chicken feet. He came back to Hal, stretched his neck up and honked bossily for her to give him more to eat.

She laughed. "Sorry, but you have just eaten all I had. That is all Emma wants the chickens to have at one time." She turned the pail over and patted the bottom to show him the pail was empty. The duck stretched his neck in an S, turned his beak upward and gave her a disgusted look out of one black eye. Then he turned his back on her and waddled away, pushing the hens out of his way to get to his foster mother.

"Plain males. Be it fowl, beast or human, they must all be born with an instinct that tells them they are in charge," growled Hal.

By the time John, Hal and Emma arrived in Elton's room, he had finished his breakfast and was napping. Jane rushed to greet them at the door. "It is gute to see you this morning."

"How is he?" Hal asked.

"The doctor has not been here yet. The nurse says Elton is resting comfortable." Jane looked over at her husband and said softly, "I have to take her word for it. The nurse did take him off that machine he was on. That must mean something gute."

"It does," Hal assured her.

"We do not want to wake Elton up. He needs all the rest he can get," John said. "You tell him we came to see about him."

"Jah, I will," Jane said.

From across the room, they heard the man's soft husky voice, "Did I hear I have company?"

Jane ushered the Lapp family to him.

John leaned on the side rail and took the man's hand. "We are here."

Emma walked around the other side and bent to give Elton a kiss. The elderly man looked from one to the other and smiled weakly.

Hal thought it best to keep quiet and stay at the foot of the bed. She noticed Elton's once ruddy completion was very pale. His face was tight from all the pain and stress of what he had been through. All in all, Elton was lucky to be alive. She didn't want to make things worse by upsetting him if he wasn't ready to see her yet.

Elton glanced at each of the of his visitors and Jane then down at the foot of the bed. "There you are, Nurse Hal. It is gute to see you. Gute to be able to see anyone at all," he joked. "I am glad you helped me last night. It was a close call Jane tells me."

Hal patted his foot. "I'm glad I was there at the right time."

"Me too," Elton said quietly. He blinked his eyes as though his lids were too heavy to keep open and dozed off.

Chapter 16

A few days later when John and Hal came home from the hospital close to supper time on the in between Sunday, Emma met them at the door. "How was Elton today?"

"Coming along all right. He may get to come home tomorrow. Then will be the hard part for Jane. She will have to keep him quiet for awhile. It won't be easy to do when he gets to feeling more like himself," Hal said, chuckling.

"Especially since it is time to harvest his corn. Maybe I should check on him often enough to sit him down before he gets any bad notions," John said. "He doesn't have many chores. Jane can keep doing them. I'll get the neighbors together to pick his corn. We always help him anyway."

"Wonderful! That should take a load off Elton's mind if you tell him that. The doctor did say he shouldn't be doing anything strenuous for quite awhile," Hal said.

"Here comes Josh's buggy. I have to leave now," Emma said, picking up her bible off the game table. "If you are not in bed when I get home, we'll talk some more. The boys have chores about done, and I left supper in the warming oven."

Emma, excited about this first outing with a boy, rushed to the courting buggy and greeted Josh Beiler as she pulled herself in. When the couple traveled down the road, Emma wasn't sure what to say so she didn't speak. It didn't help that Josh stared ahead of the horse as if she wasn't in the buggy with him. This silence wasn't a comfortable situation like teasing back and forth with Levi Yoder always was. She could say anything to Levi. The two of them had grown up together almost like bruder and schwestern. Josh was a stranger, and suddenly a very quiet one to boot. She wished she'd had time to get to know him better before this date.

Emma was glad when they arrived at the Yutzy farm. She looked forward to being with a room full of Plain kids she knew. Her friend, Metta, dark brown hair peeking from the edges of her prayer cap, waited in the machine shed door. She waved a greeting as the couple walked toward her.

Metta kissed Emma on the cheek. Her hazel eyes lit up as she surveyed the strange boy with Emma. She held her hand out to Josh. "Ich bin die, Metta."

"Metta is our hostess tonight," Emma supplied.

Josh gave Metta his crooked grin as he took her hand. "Wie bist du bet, Metta. Ich bin die, Josh Beiler."

"It's nice to meet you, too. Wilcom to the singing," Metta said shyly as she turned and lead the way into the machine shed.

Emma added, "Josh is living with Levi Yoder's family for awhile. Since he is new to the community, he came with me to meet some folks his own age." She hoped that made it clear to Metta she wasn't going steady with Josh.

"That is gute. Josh Beiler, go over and get acquainted with the other boys," Metta suggested. As Josh sauntered away with his hands stuffed in his trouser pockets, Metta said softly, "Levi Yoder is already here." She nodded toward the group of boys.

Emma whispered in her friend's ear, "Did he come alone?"

"Jah, he did," Metta said smugly, giving her a knowing smile.

"Do not smile like a cat full of warm milk. I was just curious," Emma hissed.

In this large shed used for Enos Yutzy's farm machinery, half the room had been cleaned out so Metta could have her singing. The girls, in rainbow dresses of purples, blues and mauves, clustered in one area, talking in hushed voices. When they spotted Josh, he caused quite a stir of curiosity. The girls stole furtive glances in his direction and whispered behind their hands.

The boys in the corner were listening to one boy's tale about the stock dog he was training to bring in the milk cows. The dog was scared of his own shadow. The boy told how the dog, at the sight of a cow headed in his direction, tucked his tail between his legs and raced for home to hide. The other boys laughed.

Two long tables sat in the middle of the cleared area. Metta said loudly, "Everyone should sit down now."

The girls, not dating, sat opposite the boys at one table. The other table was for couples so they could hold hands. Josh rushed away from the boys just as Emma headed toward the singles table. He made it to Emma's side in just a few quick steps. Josh took her by the arm and twirled her around swift enough that she bumped into him.

"To this table," Josh ordered, nodding at the couples table.

Emma pulled away from him and clasped her hands behind her back. "I will sit with the girls at the singles table."

"We came as a couple," Josh insisted

"We came together so you can get acquainted with my friends. We *are not* a couple," Emma said firmly, keeping her hands behind her back.

Josh took a furtive glance around them to see if anyone was watching. Levi was paying attention. Josh didn't like the way Levi's eyes narrowed as he watched them. He shrugged his shoulders and gave Emma a surly grin. Taking a step back, he motioned toward the singles table to let her know he was giving up, but his eyes held a cool, annoyed expression.

Emma walked away from him. She sat down on the end of the bench by Katie Yost. Her hands were trembling. She gripped them tightly together under the table. Her stomach was full of butterflies. She had to gather herself and calm down. She didn't like the aggressive way Josh squeezed her arm or the distrust she felt when he took a dislike to her pulling away. When she glanced across the table, Levi was watching her closely, clearly concerned. She smiled to let him know she was fine and ignored Josh beside him.

What made her even more uncomfortable the rest of the evening was how many times Levi spoke across the table to

Katie Yost, sitting next to Emma. The two of them seemed to be getting along well. Too well. Emma wasn't so sure she liked the thought of Levi being that friendly with other girls.

Girlish chatter buzzed at the tables mingled with giggles. The boys talked and chuckled as the snack was served. There were sandwiches and cookies along with Metta's mother's good homemade root beer.

Once the singing began, some of the couples at the other table wandered outside or into a dark corner to be alone. Emma watched a couple disappear into the darkness beyond the machine shed door. She blushed at thoughts of why they went outside. When she looked across the table, Josh was smirking at her. Emma felt a serge of anxiety flood over her. It was something in his eyes. Suddenly, she dreaded the thought of riding home with him. She'd sure be glad to get this night over with.

When the singing stopped and everyone went to their buggies, Josh acted as though nothing had happened between them. His eyes were as dark as the night and expressionless as he let Emma go ahead of him out the machine shed door. She couldn't imagine what he was thinking, and she wasn't sure she wanted to know. Knowing might make her more fearful. Josh went around the buggy, leaped in and waited for Emma to join him. He clicked to the horse to start the buggy down the dark road.

Emma hugged her side of the seat and remained quiet. Out in the open, the moon brightened the landscape. She tried to keep her mind on what was in the shadows beside the buggy. Dark humps of cattle grazed, moved slowly in a pasture. An ambling creature, probably a coon, ran across the road in front of them. The startled horse's head flew up, but he kept going.

Emma's heart drummed a faster beat when Josh pulled back on the lines and turned down the narrow lover's lane that followed along the creek.

"This is the wrong road," Emma told him, hoping he was just turned around.

"Nah, it is not wrong. I thought we could take the scenic

144

route through the trees and by the water. This road does wind back out to the road that goes past your farm, ain't?"

"Jah, but it is getting late. Too dark to even see the scenic route as you call it. Besides, tomorrow is going to be a big day. My family has to go see about a friend in the hospital. I need to get home," Emma excused, instantly nervous about Josh's sudden change in routes.

"We will be at your house soon," he assured her.

The horse's hooves echoed off the trees on either side as they traveled along the packed dirt road. The buggy wheels crunched on the rocks like gritting teeth. Leaning back against the seat, Josh grew quiet again. With the silence between them, Emma prayed the rest of the night would turn out all right for her. If only there was enough moonlight allowed through the trees so she could see his face.

Suddenly, Josh commanded, "Whoa." He pulled back on the lines to stop the horse.

Emma looked around. The trees were so close on this narrow desolate road branches almost scraped both sides of the buggy. The night turned blacker as the moon slipped behind a dark cloud. The timber was too still. She was alone with this boy she didn't know. One she wasn't sure she liked even a little bit. She tried to keep the nervous tremble out of her voice, "Why are we stopping here?"

"Thought we could just sit and talk," Josh said as he edged his arm around her shoulders.

Emma wiggled away from him, leaving his arm on the back of the seat. "I need to go home *now.*"

"We will leave soon." Josh dropped the lines and slid closer. He put his head close to her face. His breath, hot on her cheek, held a hint of sweet rootbeer. His next move was so swift he'd pressed his lips hard against hers before she had a chance to dodge. Their teeth rubbed together, and Emma's lips smarted from the hard pressure of his lips. While he had her penned to the seat, Josh ran a hand down the front of her blouse.

Emma wrenched her flushed face clear of him and slapped his hand away. She snapped, "Do not do that. Take me home now."

"Not yet. We are just getting to know each other. It is not really that late. I thought we could take this blanket we are sitting on and spread it out on the ground under the trees. Talk awhile maybe," he said with a chuckle.

"Never!" Emma hurled herself from the buggy, managed to land on her feet and sprint across the road. She bent low, running through the thick underbrush. She heard Josh's feet hit the ground. He was after her. Terrified of what would happen if he caught up to her, she raced blindly in the dark. Stumbling through overgrown thickets of gooseberry and blackberry. The sticker covered branches snagged at her clothes.

She dodged around the black forms of sprouts and trees. Lower branches hung down like bony arms, grabbing at her. The painful stings when the branches slap her face brought tears to her eyes. One branch poked her in the forehead and slid up under her prayer cap. The cap hung up. Its pins took hair as the cap flew off with the branch, but Emma didn't have time to retrieve the cap. She kept moving as she rubbed her smarting head. Brush behind her crackled almost as loud as the leaves and sticks under her feet. Josh was too close.

Emma stopped to get her bearings and tried not to pant too loud. She listened intently. The wind tore through the tree tops as if warning in angry whispers of danger. The crashing of Josh's feet tromping through dried leaves and breaking sticks roared in her ears. Somewhere in her, a little voice encouraged, "Run, Emma. Run fast."

Josh shouted, "Come back. I'll take you home if that is what you want." The wind carried his voice so that he sounded closer than he actually was. At least, Emma hoped that was the case. She took off, moving away from him.

The girl had no idea which direction she was headed but she knew she had to keep going. Her only hope was that Josh had to be more lost than she was. He didn't know this timber. She did. She had played in these trees for years in the daylight. If she could out distance him, she'd eventually find her way out.

After what seemed like forever, Emma stopped to lean

against a tree to catch her breath. The night air chilled her hot perspiring body, causing her to shiver. She wrapped her arms around herself and wished she'd thought to wear a shawl. She was winded and had to try hard not to pant too loud. If she didn't make much noise, Josh would never be able to find her in the dark. But no matter how softly she put her feet down on the timber floor, she feared every footfall hammered and echoed around her. The sounds in the timber seemed louder at night.

On a limb above her came a strong flapping of wings and then a thunderous who who who. She'd woke up an owl that was crankily broadcasting her where abouts to Josh. She had to keep moving.

When she approached, small shadowy forms leaped up and rustled out of sight. Each one made her heart pound faster. She veered off toward where she thought the creek might be, but she couldn't be certain she was going the right way. She just knew if she found the creek, she'd be able to walk along it to home without being in the open for Josh to find. Not the shortest route, but she knew better than to stick to the road. Josh would catch up to her for sure. The creek wound through several farms before it reached the Lapp farm, but what choice did she have.

Suddenly, Emma left the protection of the trees and stepped onto the edge of the road. The babbling murmur of running water on the other side the road let her know she was headed in the right direction. She looked both ways, listening for sounds of Josh's buggy. Just when she was about to cross the road, she heard what she dreaded most. The slow clip clop of hooves, soft grinding wheels and harness jangling.

Chapter 17

Emma darted off the road and squatted behind a gooseberry thicket. Josh must have found his way back to his buggy. He was coming around the road, looking for her. She had to calm herself. As dark as the night was and as dense as the brush, he'd never see her if she remained very still. Let him go on by, and she could follow his buggy toward home. If he found her now, she didn't have a clue what Josh would do to her. He might not let her go home after what he'd put her through this night.

When the buggy was even with the thicket, she picked up a familiar, soft male voice. "Emma, if you are near, this is Levi." Levi repeated those words over and over sing song like. The tone sounded much like his father's while Luke Yoder gave a sermon at a church meeting.

Emma took a deep breath. Her first intake all night that had a calming effect on her fuzzy head. It was Levi. What was he doing on this road? Why was he saying her name? Not that it mattered that much, because she trusted Levi. She'd be safe with him. Emma stood up and stepped out of the brush. She said softly so as not to scare the horse, "Levi, I'm over here."

Levi pulled his horse to a stop. He jumped from the buggy and ran to her. He grabbed her shoulders. "Are you all right?"

"Jah, but I want to go home," Emma said tearfully.

Behind her way back in the timber came a distant shout she hadn't heard for awhile. "Emma!"

The girl cringed. Her feet felt like they were frozen to the ground. "That is Josh."

"Jah! We will get away and to your house before he finds his way back to his buggy. Come on," Levi said urgently as he tugged on Emma's arm to get her moving.

She let him pull her to the buggy. On weak tired legs almost too heavy to hold her weight, she climbed up to the seat. Levi shook the lines and clicked to get the horse to trot. They moved past dark trees and bushes. Fearful of all the shadows from swaying limbs to skittering rabbits, Emma's whole body trembled. With Levi to protect her, she should feel safe, but she didn't. She wouldn't feel better until she was in her home with her family and for days to come maybe not even then.

Levi reached over and put an arm around Emma's shoulders to draw her close to him. "You are shaking like a scared rabbit."

"I am cold. That is all," Emma told him.

His arm tightened around her, lending her his warm comfort. Levi grunted. "I can tell you are scared." He felt her stiffen, getting ready to argue. "Do not fret. We will be to your house soon. Can you tell me what happen?"

"It was terrible awful scary," Emma said. She gulped to swallow a lump in her throat, trying to keep from crying before she went on. "Josh turned off on the creek road without telling me what he intended to do. At first I thought he made a wrong turn. I told him that was the wrong road so he should turn around and take me home. He said he was not going to until I stayed with him. We should get out and sit on his quilt under the trees. I did not like the rough sound of his voice. I jumped from the buggy and ran into the timber." She looked over her shoulder. "He came after me, but I was too fast for him. I think he is lost in the timber and can not find his way out."

"Voonderball gute for him," Levi said sarcastically. "I hope he stays lost for a gute long time. Maybe this will teach him something."

"That he is dumber than a fence post?" Emma retorted.

"Not so sure about a fence post, but Josh Beiler is dumb if he thinks he can out smart Emma Lapp," Levi praised.

Emma knew he was smiling even though she couldn't see his face. "You will never know how glad I was to see you. I was not looking forward to walking the rest of the way home in the dark with him after me. How is it that you came along to rescue me?"

"I was following you. When I could not hear Josh's buggy on the blacktop ahead of me anymore, I turned down the creek road, thinking he might have brought you this way. I did not like the way he acted toward you at the singing. He is not to be trusted alone with any girl, I think, so I was worried about you."

"I know now it is true Josh can not be trusted to be nice to girls. I wish I had seen that about him before I went with him to the singing. It would have saved me from a horrible night," said Emma, uttering a regretful sigh.

"When I found Josh's buggy empty, I stopped to check out the area. That is when I heard Josh calling for you from deep in the timber. You did not answer him back. I guessed what had happened. I was not worried about you exactly. I knew you would not get lost for very long in the timber we played in."

Emma smiled weakly. "You think not? Even as dark as it is in those trees?"

"Jah. I thought if I followed the road and called to you softly you would answer. I just prayed he had not harmed you in any way," Levi said.

Emma heard the worry in his voice. "Denke, Levi. You are truly a life saver. Do not worry. Josh did not harm me. He might have, but he did not get the chance," she said, touching her bruised lips.

"I want you to know you will not have to worry about Josh trying this again. I will talk to my father about this matter. When Josh comes home, he will be sent on his way," Levi said angrily.

"Oh please, Levi, I do not want a fuss made about this matter. Please do not tell Luke," begged Emma.

"Why not?"

"This sort of thing gets twisted up when retold. You know very well the easiest thing to get for a girl but the most difficult thing to get rid of is a bad reputation. You know that is how it is. Somehow the talkers will see that I come out looking bad for being out here with Josh this late. It will be all my fault. If we keep quiet, it would be better for me. This would look bad to my father. I do not want Daed to keep me from going to singings because of one rotten boy."

"That will not happen. Your father will understand. He trusts you. What about Josh? He will not give up on you now for fear you will get him in trouble," Levi warned.

"I know how to keep my distance from him. He will never get me alone again," Emma vowed.

"What about the next innocent girl he takes for a buggy ride? You know what will happen to her. She may not get away from him as easy as you did," predicted Levi.

"I will warn the other girls not to have anything to do with Josh. The girls will not say anything to anyone else," Emma said.

"You are too upset to think clear. I do not want Josh living in our home with my sisters. They will be in danger. I can not watch him every minute," Levi declared. "I am going to tell my daed about this."

Emma heard the voice of reason coming from Levi and relented. "Do what you think is best. I do not want what happened to me to happen to Jennie or little Rose."

When they pulled into the Lapp yard, a light shone dimly from the living room window.

"Someone is still up!" Emma groaned.

"Maybe your folks just left a light on for you," Levi said hopefully. "Do you want me to go in with you?"

"Nah, I will be fine. I just do not want to face this thing anymore tonight. I will deal with it in the light of day," Emma said. She leaned over and kissed his cheek. "Denke for coming to my rescue."

She hopped out of the buggy and ran up the porch steps before Levi had a chance to respond. Gently, she turned the knob. She opened the front door as easy as she knew how, trying to keep the hinges from squeaking. In the glow of the lamp, Emma saw Hal in the rocking chair. The dim yellow light played across her prayer cap and copper red hair. Her head was tucked down to her chin. Emma hated to wake her, but she should be in bed. Hal needed her rest now that she was having a baby, and she was bound to have a stiff neck in the morning.

"Mama Hal, wake up." Emma patted the sleeping woman's shoulder.

Hal's head jerked. "Oh my, I went to sleep, didn't I?"

"Jah, and it is way past your bedtime," said Emma, trying to smile.

Hal appraised Emma from the top of her head to her feet and finally studied her face. "It must be late. Did you have a good time tonight?"

"Jah, the singing was fun."

Hal's eyes narrowed. "Are you all right?"

"Tired is all. You should be, too," Emma said.

Hal stood up and moved close to the girl. She gently picked a couple of leaves from Emma's hair. "Where's your prayer cap?"

Emma put her hand to her head and felt around. "I must of lost it somewhere."

"Was Josh driving the buggy that fast?" Hal asked in concern.

Emma studied her shoes. "Nah, but the breeze is gusty. It was Levi that brought me home. You know he never goes very fast."

Hal pelted Emma with questions. "Levi brought you home? You went with Josh. What happened to Josh?"

"I am not sure," Emma said softly, not looking up.

"What aren't you telling me?"

"Ask me no more questions, Hallie. You will not like the answers. Now we should be in bed. It is late, and I am ferhoodled from the singing tonight. Hurry. Let us get under the covers." To be sure Hal didn't ask anymore questions, Emma raced up the stairs to her room and closed the door.

Hal watched the girl disappear as fast as a frightened deer. Emma certainly seemed nervous, and what could she say that

152

Hal wouldn't like. Something went wrong on her date, but what? Had she dreamed it or did Emma call her Mama Hal when the girl woke her up? Emma didn't usually call her anything other than Hallie. Emma's night out at the singing had not gone well. That was clear. Did she have a disagreement with Levi? That was hard to believe. That boy would never do anything to upset Emma. Josh, on the other hand, was a different tale. Why hadn't he brought Emma home? Could the reason have something to do with Emma's disheveled appearance? Not much chance she'd find out until morning, and Emma was right. It was late in the night. Way past both of their bedtimes. The main thing was Emma was home safe. Tomorrow was time enough to get the story out of her.

The next morning by the time the sun created a golden glow over the countryside, the Lapp farm bustled with activity. The boys were in the barn helping John milk. The rumble of the generator was loud as it pulled the milk through the lines and into the bulk tank. Cows bawled impatiently, wanting their turn. Horses nickered to each other, and the hogs squealed.

Noisy outside was quite different from the quiet kitchen. As Hal came into the room, Emma darted a glance her direction. She continued to fill the coffee pot, place the dipper in the water bucket and hustled to the stove.

Hal had the morning routine down pat so she didn't need to be told to get the bowl of eggs from the counter and place it on the warming oven. She broke eggs into the heated iron skillet. Together the two of them made fast work of getting breakfast.

For awhile there were only a few short words between them. Finally, Hal couldn't take not knowing what happened. She asked, "You seem really quiet this morning. How are you?"

Just as John and the boys entered the kitchen, Emma mumbled, "I have been better." She turned to her father and said, "Wash up. Breakfast is ready."

As they sat down at the table, a horse nickered shrilly. Someone shouted whoa as a buggy grated to a quick halt in the driveway. Noah jumped up and looked out the window. "It is that Josh fellow. He is calling awful early, ain't he?" He turned to grin at Emma.

His sister's face turned white. Poised to flee, she clasped her trembling hands tightly together. "Excuse me. I have to go to my room. I do not feel gute." She rushed out of the room. Her hollow steps pounded up the stairs.

Josh tromped across the porch and banged persistently on the door. John rushed to let him in with the others behind him. Hal looked toward the top of the stairs. Emma was out of sight, but Hal caught a glimmer of her green skirt at the hallway bend.

When Josh rushed inside, Hal stared at the mess of a young man. He had his hat against his heaving chest. His clothes were disheveled. Leaves in his hair and plastered on his shirt just like Emma the night before. His shoes were covered in red mud, and he was holding out a bible for one of them to take. "You must come help me find Emma before it's too late," he said hoarsely.

Taking the bible, John puzzled, "This is Emma's. Help you find Emma you say?"

"Jah, I have looked all night. She is lost in the timber that runs along the creek road. I was lost myself until just a little bit ago. I shouted and shouted until I was not able to say the words loud enough for Emma to hear me. She did not ever answer me." The husky words rushed out of his mouth as he leaned on the door facing.

Hal said in a let me get this straight tone, "You took Emma to the singing. That is not the way home from the Yutzy farm or any other. Why would Emma go in that timber after dark by herself?"

Josh was taken aback by Hal's accusing voice. He stuttered sullenly, "We --- we pulled off the main road. I got lost."

John pressed, "Emma knows the way home. She would have been the first to tell you there is no way to get lost on that road. The road comes back out to the main road and heads this way. If Emma was lost in the timber, she had to get out of your buggy."

"Why if this happened last night, did you wait until now to

154

tell us Emma is missing? We should have been out there with you, helping hunt for my schwestern." Noah demanded, his arms folded over his chest as he glared at Josh.

"Jah, that is right," added Daniel.

"I told you I was lost in the timber myself. I just found my way out," Josh insisted, shifting his eyes from person to person.

"Why would you take my daughter into a timber late at night?" John demanded.

"We -- we were just going to go for a walk," Josh stammered.

"Why didn't the two of you stay together so you could protect her?" Hal asked.

Bombarded by so many questions, Josh opened his mouth to speak, but he couldn't come up with answers that would keep him out of trouble with the Lapp family. He inclined his head and shrugged his shoulders instead.

From midway on the stairs, Emma calmly accused, "I can answer for him, because he is lying."

They all turned to look up at her.

Surprised, Josh exclaimed, "Emma! You are all right. It is voonderball gute that you are all right. How did you find your way home?"

"I was rescued by Levi Yoder. He knows the truth. If I were you I would not want to go back to the Yoder house with this story. Levi and his father are not going to treat you kindly, and they will not accept a lie," Emma warned with steel in her tone. "Now leave here and never come back."

Josh backed out the door and shut it. They could hear him running to the buggy.

John turned to Emma. "Come down here and talk to Hal and me. Boys, go eat your breakfast."

Curious, Noah and Daniel trudged into the kitchen heavy footed. Noah whispered in Daniel's ear, "Do not worry. We will find out what happened later."

"Sit down here," John said, pointing to a chair.

Emma did as she was told and explained what had happened

the night before.

Hal said, "I knew something was wrong. Why didn't you just tell me when I asked?"

"I did not want to worry you. When Josh found his way out of the timber, I thought he would go back to the Yoders and keep quiet. Maybe he would pack up and leave if I was lucky. I told Levi to not say anything about this, but he didn't want Josh Beiler in their home after what happened. I was afraid the story would not be told in my favor. I did not want that. I did not want Daed to think I could not be trusted to go to the singings just because I am a poor judge of people," Emma told her.

"I will always believe you. I know what happened was not your fault. Keeping still is no excuse for not telling us the truth," John said sincerely.

Emma sighed. "I know that now. Levi told me you would say as much. I suspect something like this has a way of coming out whether we want it to or not."

"You said a mouth full," Hal declared, thinking about the trouble she was in because of her car and phone.

"Who knew Josh had enough of a conscious that he would come for help to find me," Emma said.

Hal shook her head. "Emma, Josh was only thinking about himself."

Emma couldn't understand. "Mutter Hal, wie waar des?"

"How it was is simple. All that boy did by coming here was try not to get in anymore trouble than he was already in for taking you down the creek road. He knew it was wrong to take you there against your will. His intentions weren't good ones. If he left you out there in the timber to die of exposure, he'd have been a murderer. He felt he had no choice but to get help to find you after he didn't have any luck on his own."

"I see," Emma said sadly. It was all clear to her now. The innocent trust she thought she'd always have for people in her life had been shattered like thin ice on a thawing pond. She had learned a valuable lesson about trusting her own gut instincts where people were concerned.

Chapter 18

On Monday morning, Hal went to visit Elton in the hospital. After she found out he'd been released, she offered to take him home, but he refused. He said he'd wait for Jane to come in their buggy. He'd been pacing around his room to get exercise. Hal thought he seemed strong enough to stand the carriage ride so she didn't try to persuade him to pick a different method to get home.

A couple days after Elton had time to get used to being home, the Lapp family went for a visit after supper. As friendly to her as the Bontragers seemed, Hal was nervous about being in the same room with Elton now he'd gotten most of his strength back. So far he didn't seem to have giving her a lecture on his mind. Right now he was just glad to be alive. He was happy to see the whole Lapp family including Hal.

Once Elton felt better, his mind turned to fall field work, and he didn't like the idea of staying in the house. He asked John how the harvest was coming. John told him they were going to start on his corn field in the morning.

"Gute, I feel like helping now," Elton said.

"Oh, Elton," Jane protested.

Elton gave his wife a hard look, and she didn't say anything else.

John said bluntly, "We do not want you to help this year. Your neighbors will harvest the corn. You need to get gute and well before you try working again."

"I am doing all right," Elton protested.

John shook his head. "You will do even better at getting well if you are watching from the window this time. The doctor said you need rest and a chance to give your heart time to heal. We do not want to stop cutting your corn to take you back to the hospital because you are having another heart attack. You have helped many farmers when they needed it. Now it is their turn to help you, and they are glad to do. Think about it, Elton. If you ever saw a frog sitting on top a fence post, you know it did not get there by itself. It had help," John advised.

"All right," Elton gave in. "Just call me Goliath." He winked at Daniel, sitting by Hal. Elton got out of his chair and walked over by Hal's chair. He picked up her hand from her lap. She dreaded what was coming. "And as for you, Nurse Hal, you seemed to be the lady that put me on that fence post." His voice held a pretend sternness before he broke out in a smile. "I am so grateful to be alive today. I want to tell you denke."

"Oh, Elton, you are very welcome," Hal said. "I'm glad I was here when you needed me." She stood up and gave him a big hug. She knew the inevitable was going to happen sooner or later, but she was just as glad it wasn't at that moment.

Later the next afternoon, John stopped at the Bontrager house to tell Elton how the harvest was going before he went home to milk.

"I watched from the window as the shocks went up across the field. All the time, I wished I could be out there helping my friends in my cornfield," Elton admitted.

"Not this time, Bruder Elton. Remember you are the frog on the fence post for awhile," John said grinning. "I catch you out in that field, and I will tell Nurse Hal on you."

Elton nodded but he didn't smile. He studied his hands with his mind already somewhere else.

"You for sure feeling all right? Is there something wrong?" John asked.

With slumping shoulders, Elton managed to say the words but they were like pieces of heavy lead stuck to his tongue, "Stella Strutt was here this afternoon. She said she came to see how I was doing. In truth, she heard about Nurse Hal taking me to the hospital in her car. She wanted to know if I have made a

158

decision about punishment for Nurse Hal since she continues to use her car."

John grimaced. "Stella should be more considerate of you when she knows you have not been feeling pretty gute. She is like an old dog with a bone. She is going to growl over it and chew on it until she has gnawed all the gute away."

"Jah. For sure, Stella is the watchdog of our community. She noses around for wrong doing all the time. John, she is pushing me to take a stand."

"Have you?"

"Jah, Nurse Hal should come see me about this matter tomorrow night. I need to talk to her so she is prepared. She must be in church Sunday for a member meeting. She needs to make her things right before God and the church members. I fear Stella is spreading the word about how Hal keeps breaking the Ordnund rules. I am well enough to be at the meeting this Sunday. We must not put this off any longer for Hal's sake. I know she is fretting about this," Elton said gravely. "If Jane is right about what she suspects, and she usually knows the signs when she sees them, Hal should not stay so worked up."

John cocked his head to one side. "If Jane thinks Hal is going to have a baby, she is right."

"We are glad to know this news," Elton said, smiling.

John pulled his straw hat off and ran his fingers through his hair as he stared out the window at the cornfield. "Elton, sometimes, I wonder if I'm up to the kinds of difficulties that comes with being an Englisher's husband. The English temptations she was raised with will be as hard to get shed of as burrs in a horse's hair."

"You have a gute wife. She is an asset to this community, John Lapp. Do not give up on Hal. She will learn our ways. Remember the gem cannot be polished with friction, nor the man perfected without a few trials," the bishop said sagely.

"Think there will ever come a day, my gem of a wife will be at least polished enough that we can live in peace and harmony so that my trials will not be so great? I long for that," John told the bishop sincerely.

159

Elton looked at the doorway and spoke softly so Jane couldn't hear him from the living room. "In secret, I can advise you I am thinking that day never comes completely for any married couple." He chuckled and winked at John.

That evening, John hated to tell Hal about his talk with Elton but she had to prepare herself. After the kids went to bed, he blurted out, "Bishop Bontrager wants to see you at his house. He needs to talk to you tomorrow evening about you going before a member meeting at church Sunday."

When Hal stiffened her back, John braced for her angry words, but she said quietly, "All right. Actually, I'm glad the time has come. I've been waiting for this to happen and worrying about it for too long. I've done something wrong several times over so just saying I'm guilty is not enough atonement. That is part of this Plain life I wish to live. I'll take my medicine and learn from my mistakes."

John sighed in relief. Hal was trying to understand their ways. "This is one of the reasons why I love you. I appreciate how hard you are trying to conform. I know living with our ways is not easy for you right now," John said and he kissed her.

The next day, John left right after chores to finish Elton's corn harvest. He'd be gone all day. Hal said she needed to keep busy so she wouldn't have time to worry about the member meeting. Emma suggested they pick through the red delicious apples stored in the basement and can some. Peeling the apples took most of the morning and cold packing the jars took part of the afternoon. They cleaned up the kitchen to the tune of ping, ping, ping as the jar flats sealed.

"Hallie, we're going to have to get your wedding gifts out of the closet and put them away one of these days," Emma told her, still looking for something to keep Hal busy.

"I've been thinking about that. Every gift I received we already have at least one of in this well stocked kitchen except for my beautiful quilt and cedar chest. Right?"

"I think so," Emma said slowly, wondering where Hal was headed with this.

160

"When you leave me to start a home of your own and take your hope chest with you, I'll be left with the wealth that's already in this kitchen. Right?" Hal asked.

"Jah, what is here is yours. You married Daed."

"All right. Why don't you take all those gifts in the closet and put them in your hope chest. You can have them to stock your kitchen," Hal said.

"I do not think that will work, Hallie. Will it?"

"Who is to know but me and you. I want you to take those things with my blessings," Hal assured her. "You know I don't need them, but you will."

The sudden rumble of the generator broke the silence. Noah and Daniel were in the barn, getting ready to start evening chores. Hal looked out the kitchen window. A billowing gray cloud of dust rose on the road a quarter of a mile away. Was it a whirlwind or did she hear the sound of a racing horse. She walked out on the front porch.

"Emma, come here," Hal called as the buggy appeared out of a dust cloud and raced down the driveway. "Who is that?"

"Hamish Yost," Emma said, frowning. "Must be something terrible wrong. Hamish would never run his horse."

The man pulled the winded horse to a stop near the house. He jumped down and rushed at Hal who ran to meet him. "I need help terrible fast. Nurse Hal, get me John Lapp."

"What's wrong?"

"My son, Jonas, is caught under our corn binder. He is screaming terrible awful. The sickles cut him. He's bleeding real bad," Hamish said, choking on the words.

"Anyone with him?" Hal asked.

"David Bender and Laverne Keim. I hired them to help us with the corn harvest. We can not lift the binder off Jonas by ourselves. We need help," Hamish said, choking on the words. "Is John Lapp home?"

"No, he is over at the Bontrager farm harvesting Elton's corn. I'll send for him and the other men helping him. Wait a minute while I get my nursing bag." Hal rushed to the table in the clinic and grabbed her bag. She opened a cupboard door

161

and swiped a couple boxes of different size gauze into the bag.

As Hal ran across the driveway to the barn with Emma behind her, she said over her shoulder, "You and I will go help Hamish's son." She shouted in the barn door, "Noah, come quick." When the boy appeared, she said, "There has been a farm accident at the Yost farm. Hamish needs our help. Hop on a horse and race over to Elton's cornfield. Tell your father Hamish's son is penned under their corn binder. Men are needed to lift the binder off him. Emma and I are on our way there."

Hal rifled through her nursing bag for her phone. "Get in the car with me, Hamish. We can get there so much faster than in your buggy. Your horse is worn out."

"I can not," he faltered.

Hal paused with her hand on the door handle. She didn't have time to debate with Hamish the sinful risks of riding in the same car with her. "Won't you ride in back? This is the fastest way to get help to your son."

Hamish hesitated a second. "Jah," he agreed and climbed in.

Hal started the car and dialed 911. "Hallie Lindstrom, Home Health nurse. There is a machinery accident at the Hamish Yost farm. A man was caught under a moving corn binder and cut numerous places by the sickles. He's losing a lot of blood."

"Ambulance will be on it's way. Need a rescue airlift?"

"Sure sounds like it. I'm on the way to the scene. We will need plenty of help to lift that heavy binder off the man. I've sent for my husband and some other farmers to meet me at the field. From what the father says, the man's injuries are extensive."

"A deputy is out your way. I'll head him to the farm," the dispatcher told her.

Hal sped down the road, hitting almost every pothole and leaving a cloud of dust in her wake. She could clearly imagine what the young man looked like when she thought about the clattering binder sickles slicing through him as they did the corn stalks.

Emma twisted in the front seat and asked of Hamish, "How

did this happen to Jonas?"

"A fox ran out of the corn rows in front of the horses. They spooked and took off. Jonas had a gute hold on the lines. The horses jerked him off the seat and over into the binder's path. The horses pulled the binder right on top of my son," he said, barely able to get the words out. "Before we could settle the horses down, my son was cut all over as the binder drug him with it."

A fearful feeling ran through Hal when she thought about the day she watched John run the corn binder. The same thing could happen to him. Horses were so unpredictable.

Following Hamish's directions, Hal soon turned off the road into his cornfield. Across the flat land to the east, she saw the ambulance miles away, coming from Wickenburg. The siren wail was faint as it raced along the black top. She stopped the car back from the binder so she'd be parked out of the emergency vehicle's way.

John, Samuel, Luke and Levi were already standing by the binder with two other men. John frowned at her car when Hal climbed out with Hamish in tow, but she didn't have time to worry about being in trouble again. She had work to do. "John, how did you get here so fast?"

"We rode our horses across the fields." He pointed to the line of red horses tied to the fence.

The sight of all those hoof stomping animals tied up made Hal nervous. She didn't want any more horse accidents right away. "There's a helicopter going to light in the field, and the ambulance coming with its siren blaring. Also, a sheriff car will be screaming in here any minute. All that noise, emergency equipment and people rushing around will likely scare those horses."

"You sent for a helicopter?" John looked troubled at yet another transgression on her part.

"Not me. It was the decision of the 911 operator when she heard what the accident was," Hal said, hoping that explanation would suffice.

Jonas cried out in pain. John glanced at the binder and said

163

under his breath, "All right, what happens here is Hamish's decision to make. It is his son that is hurt." He turned to Levi. "Turn the horses loose from the fence right away so they can run free until after we are done here." He said to Hal, "What do you want us to do?"

"Right now we need to get the binder off Jonas so the paramedics can work on him. Are there enough men here to lift the binder and sit it off to the side?"

"We will do it," John said with determination.

"Let me see the injuries first." Hal hadn't been able to see Jonas from the back of the binder, but she'd heard his painful cries. The other men paced helplessly around the binder, wanting to help and not sure what to do. Emma was already on her knees, patting the young man's leg. Hal knelt between the rows and moved Jonas's leg off a corn stab. "Jonas, this is Nurse Hal. Help is on the way. We are going to get this corn binder off you now and get you to the hospital as fast as we can."

He squalled, "Please hurry. It hurts so terrible awful."

Emma swallowed hard before she said, "We know."

"Pray for me," Jonas groaned.

"John, what is the best way to lift the binder?" Hal asked.

"By lifting on the tongue, we can bring the front end up. We'll have to pull Jonas out," he answered.

Hal turned to the men. "Two of you take hold of Jonas's legs. Emma and I will be ready to get his shoulders so we can carry him away from the binder as gently as possible. Emma, let's pray like he asked. Speak good and loud so Jonas can hear us." Hal started the Lord's Prayer in Pennsylvania Dutch, "Unser vater der du bist im himmel, geheiliget werde dein name zu komm, uns dein reich, dein viille geschehe auf, erden vie im himmel, gib uns heit.

Emma joined in, and the men chanted the prayer as they surrounded the binder tongue. Luke and John bent over Jonas's body and each took a leg and put a hand under his waist.

Hal stopped praying to say, "John and Luke, watch out for these corn stabs. We don't want Jonas lying on them after we move him. You other men, lift the binder together on the count of three. One, two, three. Lift!"

Their faces masks of wincing grimaces, the men strained and grunted. The binder rose up off the ground. John and Luke tugged on Jonas's body until Emma and Hal could get his shoulders and help lift him to safety. The movement made the young man's pain more intense. His screams caused everyone there to hurt for him.

The men set the binder down and backed up to give Hal room to work. She knelt in the dirt with her bag and searched for a packet of sterilized gloves. While she tore into the packet and put on the gloves, she shoved the bag at Emma and told her to hunt for scissors. Emma handed the scissors to Hal and took Jonas's limp, blood covered hand. Though she didn't want to look, the girl stared in wide eyed dismay from her blood stained hand to Jonas's horrible wounds. She had to watch Hal if she was going to be a nurse.

Hal cut away the tattered shreds of the man's shirt hanging from his bloody body to keep the material from drying in his wounds. She stuffed gauze in the many gashes and holes in the man's chest where areas of skin and flesh had been sliced away. She plastered gauze on his face to slow the blood pouring from where his nose used to be. Pieces of flesh lay back in slabs, exposing cheek bones on both sides his face. No sooner had Hal placed gauze on all the open areas then she started covering all the bloody gauze with a layer of clean ones.

The ambulance screamed in the gate hole with a deputy sheriff car skidding to a stop behind it. Over the farm house came the vibrating rumble of chopper blades. The helicopter circled and landed in the picked field behind the binder.

The paramedics moved in, their life saving equipment and stretcher ready. With a count of three, they lifted the moaning man onto the stretcher and walked as fast as they could in the unlevel field to the chopper. They leaned low under the slowly whirling blade as they placed the patient inside. Within moments, the helicopter rebbed up and rose, headed in the direction of the hospital.

Hamish said, "I want to go with my son."

Hal turned to John and her eyes met his warily. "I have to help him."

John nodded. "Do what you need to do."

"I don't know how long this will take. Elton wanted me to come see him tonight," Hal reminded John.

"I can explain to Elton. He will understand," John said adamantly. "Go now. Quick!"

Chapter 19

"Hamish, get in my car. I'll take you to your son," Hal insisted, taking the man by his elbow. "We can stop at the house and pick up your wife."

"She is not well enough to stand what is happening to Jonas. Cancer."

"Does she know what happened?" Hal asked.

Hamish nodded as he watched the helicopter grow smaller in the distance. "Jah, I told her about the accident before I hitched the buggy up to come get you."

"Emma, would you like to stay with Mrs. Yost until we get back? I can drop you off at the house so you can comfort her. The time will pass slow for her until her husband comes home," Hal said.

"Jah, I would be glad to do that," the girl agreed.

The hospital parking lot was busy when they arrived. Hal found one opening near the end of the parking place. Once inside the building, the ER nurse, Lucy, greeted them. "Hi, Hal. Can I help you?"

"The binder accident victim that just came in is mine. What's happening?" Hal asked.

"He's been rushed to surgery. I'll check, but it's really too soon to know much. They are probably still prepping him," Lucy said as she rushed away.

Hal lead Hamish to the waiting room. "We can sit here until we hear."

"I can not sit. I am too ferhoodled to be still." He said to her, running the brim of his straw hat around and around in his hands.

"I know what you mean. Me, too. All right, we'll walk together," Hal said patting his arm. She paced back and forth across the room along side Hamish. They walked from the line of chairs to the television perched on a shelf attached to the wall and back.

The time passed slow. Maybe because Hal kept looking at the clock on the wall too much.

"It is taking a long time," Hamish stated.

"Yes, but that is to be expected. Your son has a lot of injuries for the doctor to fix. Are you hungry? I'd be glad to find you something to eat," Hal offered.

"I can not eat," he said sadly.

She wanted to comfort this man in some way. "How about we say a prayer for Jonas?"

"I would like that," Hamish said, kneeling down. Hal joined him in a silent prayer that the surgery was going well.

They paced again, and Hal saw the doctor coming before Hamish did. She raised a questioning eyebrow and got a solemn nod of the head. She put her hand on Hamish's arm to stop him. He went to the doctor. "Ich bin die, Hamish Yost. Jonas Yost is my son."

"Mr. Yost, I'm Dr. Stan Christensen the ER doctor. I called in our surgeon, Max Rather. We did all we could for your son, but I'm not sure that will be enough. The injuries are extensive. Your son lost a lot of blood in the field. We have him in a recovery room now. All we can do is wait. I have to be honest with you. At this point, if he survives it will take a miracle I'm afraid. Would you like to sit with him?"

Hamish had tears in his eyes. "Jah."

"I'll go with you, Hamish. We can wait together," Hal said. "Which room, Stan?"

"The end one," the doctor said.

"Come. I can show you where it is, Hamish," Hal said, taking his arm.

When they walked in the room, the sight was almost more than Hamish could bare. Most of the lacerations on Jonas face had been covered with bandages, but what skin did show was bruised and swollen. The young man laid very still. He was hooked up to an oxygen tube that hissed air from the wall into a spot under the bandage where his nose used to be. His vitals showed on a screen beside his bed each time the blood pressure cuff whined full of air. On an IV stand hung a bag of blood and another with a clear fluid coursing through the tubing to the needle in his arm.

Hamish gasped. He reached out and took his son's limp hand. Hal went around the bed and took Jonas's other hand.

"I feel so helpless, Nurse Hal," Hamish cried out.

"Just know that Jonas isn't feeling pain right now. He's young which is in his favor, but to be honest Hamish, what we need is the miracle the doctor mentioned," Hal said truthfully.

"I will pray for my son's recovery," Hamish said as he bent his head. In a few moments, he looked up at Hal and studied her face. "You look tired. You do not have to stay with us if you want to go home."

"No, I want to be with you and Jonas. It's a lonely vigil if you have to do it alone. Better that there is two of us." Hal hunted up two chairs in the corner of the room. "Here we go. We'll be here a long awhile. Let's sit down." Hamish sat and lean over the bed. He stroked the bandage on his son's arm. Hal said, "I could use a cup of coffee. How about you?"

"That would be gute. While you are gone, I will say another prayer." Hamish immediately bowed his head.

Hal went to the nurse's break room and fixed the pot. Just before the coffee finished dripping, Lucy Stineford came in. "I thought I smelled coffee."

"I needed something to do. I wish I had some food for Hamish Yost. He hasn't eaten or drank anything for hours," Hal said.

"I'll scrounge up some sandwiches from the kitchen," Lucy offered.

"That would be great." Hal poured coffee in two Styrofoam cups and headed back to the recovery room. She glanced at Jonas and immediately noticed a change for the worse. Hal handed Hamish his coffee and set her cup down. "I'll be right back." She whirled out of the room and met Lucy coming with a plate of sandwiches. "Better check Jonas. He's showing signs of apnea."

The nurse handed Hal the plate and rushed into the room. She leaned over the bed, took the man's pulse and checked his heart beats with her stethoscope. She looked up and nodded her head sideways. She said the words Hamish dreaded hearing. "I'm so sorry, Mr. Yost, your son's vitals are very weak." She looked at Hal. "Call me when you need me."

Hal nodded and sat down. "The damage was just too great Hamish."

"He will go to be with God soon," Hamish said simply.

"Yes, he will. I was taught in nursing school that the hearing is the last thing to go. Say anything you want to Jonas right now, and he'll hear you," Hal told him.

Hamish said, "I love you, my son. Go and be a servant at God's side." He ducked his head and wiped tears away with a work roughened hand.

"What Jonas asked for in the field was prayer to give him strength. Can we say the Lord's Prayer again for him while he can hear us?" Hal asked. She hoped saying the prayer would let Hamish feel like he had done all he could for his son.

Hamish began, "Unser vater der du bist im Himmlerr, Gehiligest werde dein name ju komm." Hal joined in. When they said amen, Jonas took his last breath.

"Hamish, he's gone. I'll get the nurse," Hal told him.

Lucy rushed in with Hal and tried for the patient's vitals. She shook her head. "He's gone, Mr. Yost."

"My name is Hamish. His is ---- was Jonas."

"All right. Hamish, I have some release forms you need to sign, and I need information about where to send your son's body," Lucy said.

A couple mornings later, the Lapp family left home to attend Jonas Yost's funeral. Noah did the driving. John went ahead the evening before to help dress Jonas and put him in the coffin. He stayed with the Yost family all night for the wake. Hal and the kids walked past the long line of enclosed carriages on the gravel road, parked until time to go in the possession to the cemetery. Each carriage had a large number chalked on it. The number the hostlers put on the Lapp buggy made them twenty-fifth in line.

Once in the house, they were lead into the room where Jonas's coffin lay in state, held up in the air by two wooden trestles. An odor of new wood came from the coffin, wider at the shoulders than it was at the head and feet. The lid was closed. The bench wagon had been parked close by and the benches unloaded in the house for the funeral service.

Once the viewing slowed down, Elton Bontrager and Luke Yoder walked up by the coffin. She worried that the emotional stress might be too much for him, but he was a man with a sense of duty. He had been chosen bishop. Hal had the feeling only his own death would keep him from performing his duties.

After everyone sat down, the family took their seat on benches to face the coffin. Bishop Bontrager started the service. He talked about the creation of the world. He pointed out Adam was created from dust, and each person must return to dust just like Adam.

He opened his bible and read John 5:20, "For the Father loveth the Son and showth him all things that himself doth: and he will shew him greater works than these, that ye may marvel." He continued the verses until he ended with verse 30, "I can of my own self do nothing: as I hear, I judge: and my judgment is just; because I seek not mine own will, but the will of the Father which hath sent me."

Preacher Luke Yoder read Corinthians 15 from verse 35 to the end of the chapter, including the verse, "O death, where is thy sting? O grave, where is thy victory?"

Bishop Bontrager gave the closing prayer and benediction. He sat down, and Preacher Yoder read the obituary from a sheet of paper. "We are laying Jonas Yost to rest today. He was twenty five years old. Born on the Yost family farm on May 13, 1985 and departed this earth on October 21, 2010. He has 62 relatives including his three brothers and six sisters and his father and mother, Hamish and Eliza Yost. Now, Bruders and Schwesterns, I ask that you stand and file past the coffin for the final viewing."

Neighbors, friends and relatives filed past the coffin, darting glances at the Yost family to see how they were holding up. The close relatives watched as many friends and neighbors gave them a sad nod. While the last of the viewers gathered outside, the family rose and surrounded the coffin to say their last good byes.

Hamish nodded his head when they were through, and the pallbearers picked the coffin up. They slowly walked outside and placed it on the back of a flat bed springfield wagon. They unfolded a black oil cloth over the coffin. The driver took off slow while the pallbearers got in their carriages to lead the possession behind the wagon. The carriages wound along country roads to the district cemetery. Roads that Hal hadn't used before. She was glad Noah knew where they were going.

Noah turned the carriage into the parking area and stopped next to buggy 24. The cemetery was laid out in neat rows with granite tombstones all the same size. The only difference about each stone was the name and date of birth and death chiseled in each stone. By the time the Lapp family arrived, the Yost family was standing by the open grave. Men, hats in hand, and women clustered around Jonas's family to offer words of sympathy and sorrow.

At the bottom of the grave was a rough wooden box for the coffin to sit in. Three boards lay under the bottom of the box to keep the coffin off the ground. That way the ropes the men used to lower the coffin could be pulled free afterward. The pallbearers lowered the coffin gently into the grave and pulled the ropes out. One man picked up the top for the rough box they had left lean against the mound of red dirt. He slid off into the grave and dropped the top in place. Once he climbed out, the pallbearers threw shovels of dirt onto the coffin.

A group of young people sang *"Old Rugged Cross"* while the pallbearers worked. The sweet sounds of their voices weren't loud enough to cover up the scraping sounds the shovels made, digging into the fresh pile. The first few shovels full made mournful, hollow sounds as the dirt pelted the wood and scattered.

When the grave was level full, the pallbearers stopped working until after the service. They would mound the rest of the dirt up later after the others left. The bishop stepped forward to ask the congregation to say the Lord's Prayer silently.

Afterward the mourners shook hands with the family and said their condolences. Some of the women gave Eliza and her daughters hugs. John, Hal and the children went through the line to talk to Hamish and Eliza, a frail woman with black circles around her eyes. Eliza managed a weak smile as she thanked Hal and Emma for taking the time to console her family. They moved out of the way for the next person in line. As they started back for the buggy, John stopped on the edge of a gathering of men to speak to Luke Yoder.

While her father was busy, Emma touched Hal's arm and whispered in her ear, "The boys want to know if you would like to visit our mother's grave with us?"

"I'd be honored to go with you," Hal said, feeling a burst of love for these children that accepted her so easily into their family and their hearts.

Emma led the way over the unlevel ground. The boys held Hal's hands. As they walked past the stones, the only name that Hal recognized was Roseanna Nisely's first husband, Emil Miller, the man who drowned in his well. It had been three years since Diane Lapp died, and Amish people were buried in order of their death. Diane's grave was almost at the end of the row.

They quietly looked at the grave for a few minutes before Emma said to the boys, "We should say a prayer for Mama." They knelt and bowed their heads. Hal got down beside them.

When the prayer was over, Hal patted the grassy knoll and said softly, "Don't worry about your family, Diane. They're doing fine."

Everyone made their way back to the Yost house for a simple

funeral lunch in the tent. They visited as they ate cheese and bologna sandwiches with cake, cookies and pies for dessert. After lunch, the women did the clean up while the men loaded the bench wagon.

Hal found herself drying dishes while Roseanna Nisely washed.

Roseanna put a dish in the rinse pan as she asked, "Are you very busy at the clinic yet?"

"No, not much, but I hope that gets better," Hal said, trying to sound optimistic.

"I think it will. Seems lately when you are needed it is for a real emergency like Jonas or Emil," she said, looking sad as she recalled losing her first husband.

"If that is where I'm needed, I don't mind," Hal told her.

"Those times we needed you very much. Hal, have you given any thought to using the clinic as a birthing place?" Roseanna asked causally.

"Jane asked me about that some time ago. I don't mind, but I need to do some studying on obstetrics so I'm prepared if that happens," Hal answered.

"Gute. You should study right away," Roseanna said with a slight smile.

Thinking the woman had heard something about her condition, Hal asked, "Why?"

Roseanna looked around to see if anyone was close enough to hear and whispered, "Because I will be in need of your help in a few months."

"Really! That's wonderful. How soon," Hal whispered back.

"Sometime in March."

"How about that! Roseanna, I'm having a baby in March. Our two little ones will grow up together," Hal said excitedly.

Roseanna brought her wet hands out of the dishwater and gave Hal a quick hug, sending water strains down the back of her dress. Before the other women had time to notice, Roseanna stuck her hands back in the dishwater. Hal pulled a plate out of the rinse water and dried it as if nothing had been said between them.

Later on as before, the carriages filed down the roads in all directions, going home to do chores before dark.

Luke Yoder walked back to the Lapp carriage as the family was getting ready to climb in. He said to John, "See you in the morning at Elton's?"

"Jah, we can get done tomorrow if we work at it," John said.

"Gute." Luke took Emma by the arm to keep her from climbing inside the carriage. "Before you leave, I have wanted to talk to you for some time. With the harvest keeping me busy I have let too much time pass. I want you to know Josh Beiler has gone back to Minnesota. As soon as Levi told me what happened after the Yost singing, I waited for Josh to come home. I told him to leave our community. There was no room for someone like him here."

"Denke," Emma said quietly, looking at the ground as if she would like to be swallowed up.

"It was an uncomfortable, scary thing for you to go through. I hated to hear that Josh did that to you. I am proud of the way you took care of yourself. I hope my daughters will have the notion of how to protect themselves if they are ever in your place."

"Denke for telling me this. I hope Jennie and Rose never have this happen to them. It is gute to know that Josh is no longer around for us to fear," Emma said. "Now we must all go home and say no more about this." She turned and climbed into the back of the carriage with her brothers.

Chapter 20

It was a mid October Sunday and the next church meeting day. Hal dreaded the new dawn when she woke in the wee hours of morning. She hadn't slept much through the night. Just about the time she relaxed and dozed off, she roused enough to know John eased out of bed to begin his day.

"Time to get up already," Hal mumbled, rubbing her eyes.

"You must be tired. I felt you toss and turn all night," John said as he sat down and leaned back against the bed head. "Being so upset all the time is not gute for you and the baby."

"I'm afraid. What will all those people think of me and you once the church meeting is over?"

"They will abide by what the bishop says and let us continue to live our lives. Elton could say your confession of guilt in front of him and the members is enough punishment this time. It is our way to forgive and forget no matter what the bishop decides. The worse punishment is the bann if they find you guilty. You have to know that might happen. Too many folks have seen you driving your car. If they haven't seen you behind the wheel, they have heard the stories by now. The bann is usually for six weeks. During that time church members are not supposed to talk to you, and you have to eat alone. There is not supposed to be anything happen in bed between us," John explained.

"Just for driving my car," Hal groaned as she raised up on her elbow. She cast an apologetic glance at him. "It seemed like such a little sin at the time."

John took her hand and said sternly, "The danger with a little sin is that once you commit the sin it will not stay little."

"I'm finding that out," Hal said dryly.

"Try not to get too upset. If the bann happens, not everyone will be really strict about the punishment. Your friends will still talk to you during the shunning. Just some Plain folks that obey the Ordnund strictly may want to carry the bann to the full," John warned.

"Like Stella Strutt?"

John nodded. "Jah, that one."

"How about you, John Lapp? Are you going to follow all the rules of this bann if I'm shunned?"

John ran his spread fingers through his dark hair. "For the sake of the children, they need to see the punishment carried out so they understand the consequences of breaking the Ordnund. You would have to eat by yourself."

"I see," Hal said, wiping her wet eyes on the sheet hem. "How about the behind closed doors shunning?"

John smiled weakly. "That is just between you and me. You do not tell, and I will not."

Hal nodded her head slowly. "I get it, John Lapp. That part of the shunning punishment sort of works like the bundling idea you talked me into which didn't work at all." Her eyes glistened as she said, "Can you ever forgive me for getting you and me into all this trouble?"

"Hal," John said gravely tough looking as he rubbed the back of her hand with his thumb. "I feel responsible for getting you in trouble. I consented to go with you on that trip in your car even though I knew we were wrong. As for the other times, you have used your car and the phone, I can not say what will be made out of that at the member meeting. You had been warned and still did these things. I do not want to see us suffer because of this bann. Just remember what I say now. If you disobey the Ordnund in any way in the future, what Bishop Bontrager hands down as punishment next time, I *will* obey fully. That is the way it should be."

Hal clamped her lips together tight to stop them from trembling. His stoic look told her he meant what he said. He wouldn't compromise his faith and way of life ever again for her or anyone else. She took a deep breath and answered calmly. "I agree. I am Plain now. Your way is my way, and that is the way it should be, my husband." The scent of Emma's freshly baked biscuits and hamburger gravy crept up the stairs and into the bedroom. "Now go get the chores over with. I'll go down and help Emma."

Hal had to prepare herself for whatever happened at church. It was going to take some heavy duty bolstering up, because she didn't want to face all those people. To be brought up before a member meeting was the most unpleasant experience she could think of. She hated it for herself, and she hated it for John and the kids. She was guilty of breaking a law in the members eyes. She couldn't quite believe Plain people were that much different from English people. Where she came from, they didn't seem to forget a past mistake. It could be just as hard on her from now on to live in this community and go to church with these people.

Hal was guilty of bringing this shame on her family. To add insult to injury, she'd had a double load of dread ever since Emma informed her the church meeting was at Stella Strutt's house. That was added punishment, knowing she'd be on her knees before everyone with Stella Strutt's righteous eyes boring into her back.

Hal intended to admit to making a mistake when she used the car to go to Mt. Pleasant. She'd say guilty when the bishop asked. That was a given. The hard part was not knowing how she was going to be able to spit out the word guilty when asked about using the car for taking Elton to the ambulance. She didn't feel guilty about getting to Jonas Yost as quick as she could to help him, either. Guilty was going to be a hard to say out loud in front of all those people when she didn't feel the least bit guilty for doing her job.

The Lapp family arrived at 8:30 at the Strutt farm. John pulled the carriage close to the house so Hal and Emma could get out. Noah and Daniel stayed with John to help him unhitch the horse. They parked in the row of buggies in front of the barn. Once Ben was in the barn with the other horses munching on the hay in the manger, John joined a group of men, shaking hands with each. The men talked farming as they did any church Sunday. Noah and Daniel joined the boys, but they didn't listen to the conversations. The two of them stared off into space with their hands stuffed in their trouser pockets, a glum look on their faces.

Women left their shawls and bonnets on a table by the door in the enclosed front porch. They chatted among themselves in the bedroom where they would sit during church. Hal and Emma sat down on a bench not so close to the group with the intention to wait for the morning to come and go. It would happen none too fast to suit Hal.

Some of the women moved out of the cluster to greet new arrivals. They stopped to speak to Emma, and she acknowledged their greeting. They spoke to Hal, called her Sister Hal and shook her hand as if she'd been going to church with them for years. Hal assumed these women didn't know any better than to associate with her. It was early. Wait until after the service, when everyone heard about the member meeting. When her name was called as the one to be discussed and she came forward, these women had to pass judgment on her. They would listen to the bishop as her discipline was meted out. Would these women be so friendly once they knew she'd sinned and not only once but repeatedly?

Just before 9 a.m., Minister Luke Yoder walked over to a gathering of older men and lead them into the house. This was the signal to the rest of the men and boys to follow. They entered the porch and laid their hats on an empty table.

The wide living room was filled with benches for the men and boys. The women and girls were in the bedroom just off the living room. Young women with small children went to the kitchen where they could move about without disrupting the service. When a baby cried, the mother would slip upstairs to feed and diaper the baby.

Bishop Bontrager stood up from his seat in the middle between Minister Yoder and Deacon Enos Yutzy. The congregation grew quiet as he announced the start of the

179

service. Emma reached for Hal's hand as she kept her eyes on the doorway. The bishop asked song leader, Samuel Nisely, to appoint someone to lead the first hymn from the *Lieder-Sammlung*, a small song book published in 1860. Samuel picked Isaac Briskey. Isaac told everyone the page. He began each verse, and the congregation joined in to finish it.

Once the singing was underway, the ministers rose and went upstairs. They sat in one of the bedrooms long enough to discuss who would take each part of the church service. They discussed church business and knelt in prayer. With a grave look on his face, Bishop Bontrager explained there would be a member meeting after the service to discuss punishment for Hallie Lapp. Minister Luke Yoder gave a tight lip nod, and Deacon Yutzy looked sadly at the bishop.

The next song was the familiar one that the congregation hardly needed a book to go by. Everyone knew *Lob Lied* was always the second hymn sung at each regular service. This is a praise song. The leader started with a series of Ooooo-Oo's and the others join in on "*Gott*." The length of the song would take at least fifteen minutes, depending on how slow they sang.

A third hymn was picked and bashful, young, Jake Yutzy, the deacon's son, was asked to lead. His voice trembled, but he managed to get through the first verse. When the congregation sang the second verse, it was the signal for the ministers to come back downstairs and take their seats.

After that hymn ended, Minister Yoder stood to give the Anfang, the order in which the ministers had agreed upon to do the service. Luke Yoder was first, and he gave a half hour sermon. Once he finished, he asked for the congregation to kneel in silent prayer. The congregation rose and turned around. They descended to the floor and leaned their elbows on the benches for several minutes. They rose. The men turned around, but the women didn't while Deacon Yutzy read several chapters of scripture in a book in the Old Testament.

This is the time, people left if they needed to go to the bathroom. Usually, the women in the kitchen went upstairs to unbundle their babies to checked their diapers or took their toddlers to the bathroom. Some of the children were laid on a bed for a nap. Other women let the tots lean over and sleep with their heads in their mother's laps.

The congregation sat down when the Bible reading finished. Bishop Bontrager stood to preach the main sermon. Powerful speaker that he was, he kept his eyes on the congregation to make sure they paid attention. Hal had a stabbing misery consume her when Elton looked in her direction. He studied her for a long moment. Once in awhile, he spoke scripture she thought was designated especially for her. Maybe it was and maybe not. She had no idea what Elton was really thinking about the up coming member meeting, but all too soon she was going to find out.

Most of the time the bishop tried to stay in view of the bedroom doorway so he could divide his eye contact between the men's section in front of him and the women's section. At one point, Elton concentrated on the young people in the congregation on the back benches in both rooms. He waved his hands around as he pleaded with them to live pure lives and think first of the Kingdom of God. He warned of the consequences of careless living and reminded the youth that one reaps what one sows.

Hal was sure he was using her for an example when he told a parable he said was titled *The Greedy Heifer.*

"One evening when a woman was helping her husband do chores, she decided to feed the heifers so that he would be done with his work sooner. After she fed them all, and they were eating contentedly, she walked past them with another shovel full to feed the dry cows. As she walked past, a young heifer tried to snatch a mouthful off the shovel, ignoring all the feed she had before herself.

"You silly, greedy heifer." The woman couldn't help but think. It was disgusting, really. The heifer had all the feed in front of her that she could possibly eat, and yet she was trying to snatch away some of the other cows feed.

But later on, after thinking it over, the woman had to wonder how often we are in the eyes of God like that greedy heifer.

Blessed with plenty to eat, warm houses, good homes, family and friends, and all the material things we will ever be able to use and more. Yet we look about and lament that others appear to have more than we do.

Are we in the habit of counting our many blessings and appreciating all we have, or are we often wishing for and wanting what others have? Do we find ourselves watching others or do we need to make our things right in our own lives and not worry about what others are doing?"

So sure the message was about her car and phone, Hal raised her bowed head and darted a glance at Elton, standing in the doorway. He may have been looking at her before, but he wasn't now. He was staring at Stella Strutt. The older woman had her head held high like a proud old mare about ready to rear up on anyone that came close. Right then, Hal felt appreciation for Elton's fairness. He seemed to be sticking up for her though she was sure he didn't condone what she had done so willfully against the Ordnund. He was trying to defend her just a little to Stella. It helped a tad to know that maybe Stella was in a little bit of trouble with the bishop for constantly being a thorn in Hal's side. As often as the old woman complained to Elton, she was a thorn in his side, too.

Coming close to the end of his sermon, Elton picked up a German New Testament and read the second of the chapters that had already been specified for that Sunday. He read several verses at a time, commented on them and continued on to the next ones.

Because church was at her farm, about half way through the three hour service, Stella, a stoic expression plastered on her face, passed a few bowls of crackers and glasses of water to the preschooler children. This was a welcome treat for the small ones that had sat so quietly for long hours.

After Bishop Bontrager finished his sermon he asked the congregation to kneel in prayer. This time the prayer was a long spoken one read from the *Christenpflicht*. When the prayer ended the congregation rose from their knees but did not sit down. The bishop pronounced the benediction. When the name of Jesus was mentioned all of the congregation bent at the knees slightly.

Bishop Bontrager said, "Sit down." Once the congregation was seated, Bishop Bontrager announced, "The next church service will be held at Deacon Enos Yutzy's farm. Today, there will be a member meeting with a discipline to be discussed for Hallie Lapp. After the final hymn all that are not members may be excused."

As soon as the song ended, the young people hurried out of the house. They could hardly wait to get to freedom and fresh air. They wanted to visit among themselves, and this was an unusually nice fall day. What better place to be than outside after sitting in that stuffy house for three hours.

Emma was not about to wander away from the house when the group of teenage girls motioned her in their direction. She wanted to hear first hand what the members were going to do to her Hallie. She edged around the house and sat down on the ground under the open living room window. Leaning back against the house, Emma tilted her ear toward the window. Right now all she heard was many footsteps as the members took different seats now that the young men had left. The women came from the bedroom and sat on the empty benches on the left.

Worried about Hal, Noah and Daniel searched for Emma to console them. When the boys spotted her, they slipped along side the house. Bending down, they crawled below the window to sit beside her.

"What are you doing, Emma?" Noah whispered.

Emma pointed upward to the open window. She scowled at him as she pressed a finger to her lips. "I'm going to listen to the meeting. I want to know what is happening to Hallie," Emma hissed at him.

"We would like to stay and listen. Is that all right?" Daniel asked.

"Jah, as long as you keep quiet. No more talking," Emma scolded softly. "Help me pray for Hallie."

Daniel crossed his arms over his chest and whispered

harshly, "I am going to pray for Stella Strutt's horse."

Emma looked aghast. "Why would you do such a thing?"

"I'm going to pray that the horse bites her where the sun does not shine for doing this to Mama Hal," Daniel said sharply.

Noah snickered behind his hand.

"Noah, do not encourage your brother's bad behavior. Daniel, you can not do that," Emma scolded.

"Why?"

"I only want to have to pray for one member of this family at a time. If you pray to God to hurt an old woman like Stella, I will have to pray for your forgiveness. I have not got time to do that for you. If you want to pray for Stella, pray that you can find it in your heart to forgive her for what she has done to our Hallie. You know to forgive is the Plain way. Now help me pray for Hallie," she hissed as she took both her brothers hands.

They heard Bishop Bontrager clearly say, "Schwestern Hallie Lapp come forward."

Hallie's black shoes made a hollow tap on the wooden floor. The room was so quiet it was as if no one was there but her. She wished she could pretend that was the case, but she felt the multitude of eyes trained on her. Hal walked down the aisle to the front of the room with her eyes fixed on the wall behind the ministers. She couldn't meet the eyes of anyone in the congregation. Not even John's. It was definitely going to be hard to look at the ministers until she had to.

She stopped in front of the ministers chairs and knelt down before Bishop Bontrager, Deacon Yutzy and Luke Yoder. She closed her eyes and bowed her head. With her hands hidden under the edge of her skirt, Hal hoped no one realized how shaky she was.

"It has come to our attention, Schwestern Hallie Lapp, that you have been weak and tempted to sin. The sin of driving a car to Mt. Pleasant to the Old Thrasher Reunion. Is this a true offense," the bishop said in such a rote tone that he might have just announced the next church service.

"Jah," Hal said softly. "I did that."

"By driving the car, you broke a rule in the Ordnund. So you are confessing your sin before the members and God?" The bishop asked.

"Jah, I am guilty," Hal said. She looked up into Elton's eyes so he'd see she was sincere. "I was weak. I sinned, and I'm so very sorry."

"Very well then," Bishop Bontrager said gravely. "I accept your admission of guilt and your willingness after this to conform to the Ordnund rules. I say that church members can forgive you for this first offense." He looked over Hallie's head at the church members as he said, "We *all* will move on and put this matter behind us."

The bishop cleared his throat as he continued to focus over Hallie's head. Hal wondered if he was looking at Stella Strutt. "Now for the next matter against Nurse Hal Lapp brought by a member of this church. It has been told to me that you continue to use your car and your cell phone to go to work and in the nursing aid of Plain people even now that you are one of us.

It is true the phones in the phone sheds at the intersections is allowed for use by all of us, but cell phones are forbidden. Cars are not owned or driven by Plain folks. We forbid these worldly items on purpose so that we are not tempted to become part of this other world that is not for us. When we ride in a car it is to be driven and owned by someone not Plain. We sit in the back seat. That is the rule of the Ordnund." The bishop paused and took the time to make eye contact with many of the men and women. "I've stated what we all know to be part of the Ordnund, these rules that we live by every day of our lives.

Now I ask our church members to consider the circumstances in this case before we vote to punish or not to punish Nurse Hal on this matter. I am here to say I would not be alive today according to the doctor at the hospital if Nurse Hal had not taken me in her car to the highway to meet the ambulance. By the time, Jane hitched up the buggy it may have been too late to help me. If Hal had not had a cell phone with her, she could not have call for the ambulance to meet us on the highway.

I asked some of the members of her family if Nurse Hal talks on the cell phone much at home." Hal brought her head up sharply and met his eyes as she waited for the answer. She knew John told Elton the phone battery was dead. Hopefully, the bishop had learned from his wife why that wasn't true. He went on, "I was told Nurse Hal never uses the phone by her husband, John Lapp, and his son, Daniel. I believed these gute folks when they told me Hallie Lapp kept the phone out of sight in her nursing supplies. I am witness to the fact that she used the phone when it was necessary to call for emergency help for others. Tell me, are there many among you that can say that an emergency call is all you use the phone for in the shed."

The bishop paused then added, "How many calls do the rest of you make to help others? Look at me standing here before you. I am living proof. Right now I would be dead for sure if not for Nurse Hal's phone and car. I owe God my life for sending this woman kneeling before me now to help me survive the heart attack.

Should I have refused to get in her car, knowing she would be the driver? Jah, maybe I should have, but tell me are there any among you that would refuse if you thought you were going to die. Now let each of you vote. If you believe Nurse Hal to be guilty say so. You know her punishment if we decide she is guilty. She will be put under the bann for six weeks while she considers her sins and comes to repent before us at another church meeting. In order to fully repent, she has to sell the car and throw away the phone." The bishop nodded to a man on the front row. "You first, Hamish Yost. Do you agree Nurse Hal is guilty?"

Throats cleared and feet shuffled. Everyone sounded as uneasy as a pen full of cattle waiting to be loaded in a truck headed for the sale barn. Hamish Yost cleared his throat and testified. "Nurse Hal took me in her car faster than my tired horse could pull my buggy back to my wounded son when the corn binder was on top of him. I chose to ride with her back to the cornfield. That makes me as guilty as Nurse Hal."

Hal couldn't believe her ears. Hamish was sticking up for her.

Hamish wasn't through yet. He was saying, "She has been kind to me and my family during this sorrowful accident. When Jonas was in great pain under the binder, Nurse Hal prayed loud for him so he would be able to hear her. She did that to comfort him while we pulled the binder from off him.

The helicopter, which we are not to fly in, was the only way to get my son to the doctor fast if he was to have any kind of chance at all. I did not object to my son using it. I could not. I would not have been with my son when he died if not for Nurse Hal driving me to the hospital in her car. She could have just left me there alone, but she stayed with me to comfort me until Jonas died. She brought me home in her car and comforted my wife and family. I do not agree she should be punished. My family owes her a great deal that I will never be able to repay. If she is to be punished so should I be. I say she is not guilty."

The bishop nodded at Samuel Nisely to speak next. He said in his soft bashful voice, "Nurse Hal fixed up my arm once. She is a gute nurse. I think of the car and phone as part of her nursing equipment. I do not agree she is guilty when all she thinks about is helping us when she uses these things."

David Bender spoke next. "I was at the Yost farm the day of the accident. I saw how caring Nurse Hal was with Jonas, giving him medical aide as well as spiritual aide. If I was to get hurt I want to know that she would be able to get to me as fast as she can and help me. I do not agree she is guilty."

And so the vote went through the men in the congregation. Moses Strutt managed a not guilty. Hal's looked at the board floor through blurred eyes and wiped away a tear on her cheek. All the men stood up for her.

Now it was the women's turn. Eliza Yost said in a voice full of strain, "Hamish told me when Nurse Hal took care of my son, Jonas was in great pain. He asked for prayer, and she provided it to comfort him while she nursed him. He would not have gotten that prayer from any English nurse or doctor. She would not have been able to help in his time of need if she did not have her car to get to him fast. When Nurse Hal was at the hospital with Hamish, she comforted my son in my place. That is important to me, because I was not there with him when he died. I vote not guilty."

Roseanna Nisely said clearly, "Nurse Hal tried her best to save my first husband, Emil Miller, when he drowned in the well. Afterward, she checked on me and the children often to see how we were doing. She is a very caring and needed person in this district. I vote she is not guilty."

The soft timid voice of Lizzy Leichenring said quietly, "When my son hurt his foot, Nurse Hal was afraid he might get lock jaw. She said we should take him to the doctor for a shot right away. To make it easier for me, she called the doctor's office and asked that we get in right away for the shot when we got to town. She explained what shot was needed so the nurse would be prepared. We did not have to wait for hours like we normally would. I appreciated her using the phone to help us. I vote not guilty."

Next Jane Bontrager spoke. "Nurse Hal became educated as a nurse to help others. She is gute at what she does and works very hard to help her patients. We are lucky to have her among us. Now Elton has told the truth when he said we both rode in the back of Nurse Hal's car. Everyone knows we were not invited to get in Nurse Hal's car to go on a joy ride. Elton was in a life or death situation and needed to be in the hospital quick. If not for Nurse Hal driving us to meet the ambulance, my husband would not be standing before us today. How will any of you act in a scary time like Elton and me faced? Would you send this woman away knowing that you are not going to live much longer without her medical help just because she showed up in her car? We owe her Elton's life. I vote Nurse Hal is not guilty."

Bless her heart. Jane's opinion means a lot to the members, Hal thought.

The bishop called on Margaret Yoder next. Hal pressed her lips together to keep them from trembling. What Margaret might say was a worry. Margaret could easily tell everyone that she knew about the call from Barb just before the wedding. Hal crossed her fingers under her skirt.

Margaret said, "We are much better for having Nurse Hal among the Plain people. She helps us anyway she can. She has a gute clinic at her house. We need to use that service more than our community does. I vote not guilty."

The bishop called on Stella Strutt next. Hal dreaded what was going to come out of that woman's mouth, but maybe it wouldn't matter how much Stella condemned her now. The rest of the congregation had just defended her.

Chapter 21

Stella Strutt cleared her throat and said in brassy dialect, " I have to say not guilty. Not guilty. I have been wrong about much where Nurse Hal is concerned. My sister, Eliza, told me how much Nurse Hal did for my nephew, Jonas Yost. She would not have been to the field so quick if she had to use a buggy, and she got so much help there to lift the corn binder off that poor suffering young man in such a short time, a short time. None of us could have done what Nurse Hal did for Jonas. We need her to stay among us. We need her to help us."

And on it went until each of the members had voted and each of them found Hal not guilty.

Bishop Bontrager stood and clasped his hands together. "The church members have spoken." He turned to the ministers on either side of him and asked them to agree or disagree. The men stated that they considered Nurse Hal not guilty. Bishop Bontrager said, "Let me tell you how I rule about this matter as the head of our church district. Remember when Freda Stoltz had pneumonia. The doctor said she needed oxygen for awhile until her lungs mended. We agreed it was more important that Freda have the comfort of the oxygen at that time until she was well again than to adhere to the strict letter of the Ordnund. I think this matter with Nurse Hal's car and phone is the same thing. The ends justify the means. We as a group have voted she is not guilty. I will allow the use of the car and the cell phone for Nurse Hal's nursing services *only,*" the bishop stressed. "Now this matter is never to be brought up again. The meeting is ended."

The women moved to the kitchen. John came to help Hal up

from the floor. She felt as if she was in a daze. Had she just escaped discipline or was she in a wishful dream? She looked at John through swimming eyes for an answer. He smiled as he handed her his hanky. "Things will be gute from now on."

Hal slipped her hand in John's and squeezed. "You're sure it's all right now?"

"Jah, it is," he said.

"John, help put these tables together," Samuel Nisely called.

"I got to go," he said, his face full of relief and joy.

Margaret rushed over and grabbed Hal's arm. "Come to the kitchen with me to help."

"Margaret, denke for sticking up for me. That must have been hard to do since you saw me using my phone," Hal admitted in a hushed voice.

"Not really. You did not make the call. Barb called you."

"That is true."

"It is a fine line I walked with this secret I kept from the bishop and members. You did have your phone in your pocket, but I sensed that day you knew you had been wrong to carry the phone. I took your word for it that you put the phone away. We need you as a nurse in our community. I did not want Stella Strutt to think she had influenced the members and get you taken away from us. Turns out, she had not influenced any of them," Margaret said.

Feeling a rush of gratitude to the congregation for their faith in her, Hal admitted, "I want you to know, Margaret I did leave the phone in the cupboard in the clinic that day and did not have it on me at home again. I wouldn't of had it with me when Elton had his heart attack but I took it to Wickenburg and plugged the adapter in at the home health office so the battery on the phone recharged. That is my life line to help in an emergency. It was just gute luck for Elton that I did that."

"Jah, very gute luck. None of us wanted to lose Elton," Margaret agreed.

Hal stopped walking with her. "I see Elton. I need to talk to him. You go on. I'll come to the kitchen as soon as I can." She walked over to the bishop. "I don't know what to say Bishop

Bontrager. I didn't expect so many people to stand up for me. It had to be your doing. You were the first to say good words on my behalf, and the others followed. Denke for helping me."

Elton took her cold hands between his warm ones and said in a kindly tone, "That is not so. The church members had those thoughts on their own. They waited until the time was right to tell you how they felt. You, gute woman, are making adjustments to be one of us. We have to remember how hard that is. Did you not think we could make some compromises for you in return?"

"I just didn't think I was worthy of the compromises in your eyes," Hal said truthfully. She was weak kneed from the agony of not knowing for days what was going to happen. That feeling was not going to leave her so quickly. "I see I was wrong. Tell me, would anyone think it wrong of me to give the bishop a hug."

Elton gave her a wide smile. "I dare anyone to come to me with a complaint on this matter. Relax and enjoy the rest of this day with these folks. They are your friends." He drew Hal into his arms and patted her back.

When they parted, he leaned forward to whisper in her ear, "But remember, you are not to be driving the car or use the phone for anything other than your nursing duties. I will stand against you if I am told that has happened. It would be your second offense and the punishment will be harsh. I would have no choice."

"I understand. I wouldn't put you, me or my family in that spot ever again," Hal vowed in his ear and gave him another squeeze for good measure.

The bishop asked bluntly, "Many of us work out and go to our jobs in buggies. What about your job?"

"I've asked for time off during the winter months so I don't have to be out on the road. I'll work in the months that are safe for me to travel in the buggy by myself," Hal said.

"That sounds like a gute, sensible plan," Elton agreed.

Hal smiled at him. "It was until I realized I'm going to have a baby. That means more time off for maternity leave."

"Voonderball gute news though," Elton explained. "I am so happy for you and John. I must confess Jane already suspected."

Hal said forlornly, "I'm happy to be starting a family. It's just that I feel like such a failure already at my Plain life."

"Listen to me, Nurse Hal. No woman is a failure that has as many friends as you do. I have never heard of or seen such a majority of church members stand up for any other Plain person before," Elton said sincerely.

"Denke for telling me that. It makes me feel better. Now I have to talk to the children. They've been very worried about me." Hal saw Emma and the boys on the front porch, looking in the screen door. She excused herself from Elton and went to the porch. "It's all right. I've been forgiven," she whispered.

Emma said, "We know."

"Already?"

"Jah, we listened under the window, Mama Hal," Noah said.

"I see."

"We prayed for your forgiveness, and God answered," Emma told her.

"Denke for helping me, kids. I was in a pickle for sure and needed all the prayers I could get," Hal assured them.

"We prayed hard," Daniel assured her.

"I know you did. It worked, didn't it?" Hal said, patting his head.

"I am glad our prayers worked. Maybe Emma was right. If I had made Stella Strutt mad by the prayer I intended, she might not have voted for you," Daniel whispered.

"Daniel, what was you going to pray for?" Hal asked hesitantly.

"For God to get Stella's horse to bite her where the sun does not shine," Daniel said seriously. "I will save that prayer for the next time Stella is mean to you."

"Let's hope there isn't a next time. You heard her say I was not guilty. We have to make friends with Stella so she will like us better. Now I have to go help in the kitchen. I don't know about you kids, but I'm suddenly very hungry," Hal said, giving

193

each of them a hug. She turned to find John watching her. He'd slipped outside and leaned up against the porch wall with his hands in his trouser pockets. His eyes held pride as he watched her with his children.

"Hello, John Lapp. Is everything all right with you now?" Hal said tentatively.

"Everything is fine with me denke very much, Hallie Lapp. Are you feeling better?"

She held the hanky out to him. "Well enough you can have this back. It's only slightly used. I'm settling down now that the worst is over. I'm so glad everyone was so understanding. Listen in there. That's all our friends, laughing, talking and working together. It's a wonderful world we Plain people live in, isn't it?"

"Jah, the best," he solemnly. "I got to go back in. I just wanted to know you are all right."

He went back to helping the men put the tables together. Once two benches were placed on the trestle in one spot, the women came along and placed oilcloths on that one and waited for the next one to be ready. The rest of the women worked on the meal. Baked bread, pickles, beets, cheese, pretzels, a hot noodle soup, cookies, pie, and a standard favorite, a peanut butter spread sweetened with marshmallow creme and corn syrup or molasses were the choices.

With so many members in a district and so little space in the house, the Amish ate in shifts segregated by sex. Older adults ate first and on down to the younger ones and youth in later shifts. Plain women made the rounds pouring black coffee and ice water. The meal was followed by a much anticipated social time, an opportunity for fellowship and to catch up on news in the two weeks they hadn't seen each other.

Later that afternoon, the Lapp family relaxed in their living room, eating popcorn and exchanging the news from church. Hal didn't join in. In fact, she wasn't even listening. She stared out the window by the game table. At best, all she managed was to concentrate on the ominous, charcoal gray clouds that were building behind the barn as she tried to gather herself. She had to come to grips with what had happened. The worse was over.

Problem was Hal couldn't help worrying. She wanted to feel better about the rest of her life in the Plain community, but there was a little piece of her that wondered what wrong thing she'd do next. This had been a rough time while she waited for the church members decision. She had to move on and settle in to this new life. Let what happen in the past go and learn from it but put this unsettling time behind her where it belonged. Her head told her that, but a doubt nibbled at her emotions. Could she move on and not cause herself and her family more unintentional trouble?

As if to remind her the future held a welcome event, she felt a nudge inside her. The baby had been really active after Hal sat down and relaxed. Maybe the baby could tell it was finally safe to make his or hers presence known. She rubbed her stomach to let the little fellow know she felt him or her. Her thoughts should be on this baby. Time had a way of getting away from her. She better be preparing for this little bundle of joy to arrive. March would be here all too soon, and she needed to be ready for this birth. Not only this birth, but now she had Roseanna Nisely to take care of. March was going to be an exciting and busy month for the clinic.

John touched her shoulder. "Hal." As from a long way off she heard his voice and forced herself to tune him in. He invited, "Hal, go for a walk with me. I think you and me can use the fresh air."

"You don't have to tell me twice. I'd love a walk," she agreed.

"Grab your coat. The temperature has dropped mightly," John said.

They started off across the pasture, walking in the short brown grass and angled in the direction of the picnic grove. Hal could feel the weight of her worries melting away with John's arm around her waist and their special place ahead of them. Off in the distance, the faint honking of geese on their southward flight broke the silence. Suddenly, the honks stopped. The geese must have landed on the pond for the night.

Dusk settled around the couple. Storm clouds covered the sky overhead by the time they reached the picnic grove. Dark wasn't far behind, and a definite chill had taken over. They didn't have long be by themselves. Hal sensed John brought her here so they could be alone for a reason. If he was going to have a discussion with her he'd have to get at it. It was just about chore time.

As if John read her mind, he stopped, leaned up against a tree and shoved his hands into his trouser pockets. "Hal, you have been much too quiet since we got home. Are you for sure going to be all right with this new life you have chosen?"

Hal twisted to face him. She wanted to be honest about her feelings. "I want to be."

"But?" He pushed.

"I'm just afraid I won't muster up to what you and the others in the community expect of me. What if I do something else to upset the bishop and break the rules?" Hal asked. "Are you always going to have to worry that I'll cause a problem for this family?"

"Stop being ferhoodled. I am not worried about you doing any such thing. This has been a hard time for you, but that has passed. You will do just fine from now on," John scolded softly, brushing a wisp of shiny red hair out of her eyes. "You have become the heart of this family. You gave my children and me laughter where there was none. You offered us your love when we needed you. My children can not do without you now. I know I can not do without you ever. I want to spend the rest of my life with you. Does it help to hear this?"

"Very much so. I'll promise to stop worrying if you tell me I can count on you to keep me on the right path for all our sakes. Can you do that for me, John Lapp?"

"Jah, we will work on this life of ours together," John said with a kind, loving smile.

Hal had one more question. "Do you think Stella Strutt is ever going to give me a break?"

"Maybe and maybe not. Who knows what Stella will try

next? We can not live our lives worrying about her. Can we?" John asked, trying to be the voice of reason.

Hal shivered as she pulled her coat tighter around her. "No, I guess not. What I do know is I'm committed to this life, committed to marriage with you and committed to our family, because I love you, John Lapp. Does it help you to hear that?"

"Jah, this from you helps me know we are going to be all right," John assured her.

"We better head back. It's dark, and I hear the generator. The boys are milking already," Hal said, taking his arm.

Not a leaf on the trees rustled. In the open pasture not a blade of grass twitched. The birds of day had gone quiet, and night birds had yet to wake. The atmosphere was laden with moisture as they headed home. "John, listen. It's so very still," Hal said, relishing the surreal peace on this farm she called home.

"Only two things quieter," John said and kissed her cheek. "The hour before dawn and the first flakes of snow falling gently to earth."

"I can think of one more moment of quiet. Just before the baby cries in the middle of the night," Hal quipped.

As John laughed, the storm cloud opened up and goose feather snowflakes fluttered down. Hal held her hand out. Two flakes landed in her palm and vanished into specks of icy water. She giggled, feeling happier than she had in days. Hal met her husband's warm dark eyes. She loved the way John looked at her. His words of wisdom made her feel secure and at peace. She loved everything about this man from the way he was taking charge of her life down to the way his beard tickled when they kiss.

Everything was going to work out for her and the Lapp family. She was sure of it now. Her worries had melted away just like the snowflakes in her hand.

John opened his arms, and Hal snuggled up against him as they walked. The words to a song kept running through her head. *It was a cold, dark night, and my heart melts the snow.*

About The Author

Fay Risner lives with her husband, Harold, on a central Iowa acreage along with their sheep, milk goats, chickens, rabbits and cats. They have one son, Duane. Now that she has retired from her CNA job at Keystone Nursing Care Center, she divides her time between writing, enjoying country life, gardening and fishing.

She has sold six stories to Good Old Days magazine and entered numerous short story and essay contests, placing numerous times.

Fay is an independent author. For more information about her life, accomplishments, and to keep up with her by reading her blog visit her websites
http://www.booksbyfaybookstore.weebly.com
Http://www.blogger/booksbyfay
http://www.twitter/booksbyfay

Fay Risner's books, with 12 font print, are reader friendly. Her stories have a Midwest, Iowa, small town flair or western adventure. The stories pull readers into the scenes, making it hard for them to put the books down until the end. Each book leaves the reader wanting a sequel or a series to see what happens to the characters next. Look for her fiction books with tags like wholesome, intriguing, heartwarming, mystery, romance, Civil War, western and children. Look for her non fiction books with tags Alzheimer's disease, caregivers and education.

Fay Risner Books

Nurse Hal Among The Amish Series
A Promise Is A Promise – Book 1
The Rainbow's End - Book 2
Christmas Traditions – An Amish Love Story

Amazing Gracie Mystery Series
Neighbor Watchers – Book 1
Specious Nephew - Book 2
The County Seat Killer – Book 3
The Chance Of A Sparrow – Book 4
Moser Mansion's Ghosts – Book 5

Stringbean Hooper Western Series
The Dark Wind Howls Over Mary
Small Feet's Many Moon Journey

Civil War Story In The Ozarks
Ella Mayfield's Pawpaw Militia – A Civil War Saga In Vernon
County, Mo.

Three Act Play
The Floating Feathers Of Yesterdays –About Alzheimer's

Non fiction

Open A Window – Alzheimer's Caregiver Handbook
Hello Alzheimer's Good Bye Dad—A Daughter's Journal

Short Stories

Wild West Tales
Butterfly and Angel Wings
A Teapot, Ghosts, Bats & More